The Everlasting Chains

Book One of The Justice Keeper Series

PETE THRON

Published in the United States of America

ISBN:978-1-68524-972-4

THE EVERLASTING CHAINS

Book One of

The Justice Keeper Series

Pete Thron

TABLE OF CONTENTS

PART - ONE

Dante Merrick sat in his cell, the place he'd called home for the past two years. The guard knocked twice on his cell door then slid a tray of food through the compartment in the door. Dante watched as a praying mantis jumped along the floor and suddenly stopped at his feet. It was looking at him as if to say, "I'm starving, how about, throwing some crumbs my way." He smiled and broke a piece of bread off his tray. He then extended his hand out and the large insect leapt onto it and started eating his snack. He enjoyed talking with the insect and had given him the name, Gus. He wasn't much for talking with the other inmates. After all, he wasn't one of them. Before being incarcerated, he'd been an undercover cop with the NYPD intelligence unit

Gus had become his friend and never left his side. The insect felt at home in the cell with him. Dante felt that the insect may have been a messenger from heaven. He tried in vain to keep the good in him, but the ordeal he was going through was getting the better of him as time went on. It was a constant battle within himself of good versus evil.

As the weeks went by, he kept thinking about the hell his young children were going through due to his absence in their lives. Their mother was purely evil.

In the beginning while he was dating her, she'd put on quite the performance pretending to be a kindhearted woman. He kept saying to himself. "Why, in God's name (no pun intended), did I decide to stay with that witch?" He knew the answer. She had a rack on her that most men would die for. His fathers, Michael the Archangel, and Samael the very first Seraphim/Archangel, who's also known as Lucifer, Aka (the devil), had warned him. They told him. "She's evil Dante, stay clear of her." It was too late for him; he was snared in by the flytrap between her legs.

Like his fathers, his lust for women was insatiable. His wife Mara was as close to perfect as one woman could be. She'd kept him sexually satisfied for five years. Now he was wondering who was warming her bed while he sat in his cell.

He wished he could contact his fathers. But couldn't risk the camera in his cell spotting them if they'd transported themselves inside the cell. Dante wasn't fond of the name that Samael went by in hell, Lucifer, or by the nickname his siblings called him, Luci. When his father wasn't administering pain and punishment to the sinners in hell he went by his true archangel's name, Samael. But in hell where he was the king, he was addressed by the demons as Lucifer.

Several decades ago, Michael and Samael decided to take a vacation from heaven and hell. The two archangels wanted to see what all the hoopla was about the humans their father adored. Michael had always questioned his father's decision not to wipe out humanity after the incident in the Garden of Eden.

Lucifer and Michael had never agreed on much, and like many brothers, they were always fighting. You can imagine their surprise when a tiny firecracker of a woman ran in front of them and tried to steal their cab.

Carolyn Merrick had angered and intrigued them both, and they'd offered to share the cab with her. The two had the same ulterior motive, to find out more about her.

Once they discovered where she worked, they began their usual competition to win her over, neither expecting to fall in love with the beautiful human. Once it happened, they'd agreed to love her unconditionally and put aside their differences with each other. Carolyn had seen both sides of Samael/Lucifer. He wanted her to see the beautiful archangel he was and the demon side. When he transformed into Lucifer it had terrified her at first. But his soft voice and gentle touch assured her, she was safe and he'd never harm her. Both archangels were strikingly handsome and had herculean physiques.

By chance, or by God, their father's meddling, he decided to teach them a lesson. One rainy night they'd both spent time with her. One thing led to another, and they both ended up in her bed at different times of the evening. Something miraculous happened. Their seeds had combined inside her and made the first Archangel-Human hybrid a Nephilim. Not that being their son had made much difference in Dante's life.

After the initial shock and confusion had worn off, the two brothers had devoted their lives to the child neither had expected to conceive. Over the years, both the archangels trained him in the Angelic ways of Heaven and Hell.

Michael, as the commander of Heaven's army, and the leader of the forces of good. He concentrated on Dante's battle skills. Since his position also required him to pass judgement, he taught Dante logic and reason, though it often went in one ear and out the other. Michael knew his son would be extremely powerful and hoped to offset some of the traits he inherited from his co-father.

Many people think Samael/Lucifer is evil. The truth is, Lucifer had grown tired of being the angel of torment and torture. His ambition to ascend and be more like his father pushed him to argue with God once too many times.

God had been having some problems with the underworld and decided Samael would be perfect to handle the situation. He decided Samael could take his light to the darkest pits of hell and see how he liked it there. He was the most powerful, and the first archangel/ Seraphim ever made. He was God's favorite, that's why he was chosen for the mission in hell.

Samael ranked the highest of all the archangels because he was of the Seraphim bloodline. Seraphim angels are the highest-ranking and most powerful angels in heaven. Samael loved the idea of having brothers and being a defender of heaven. He was fascinated with all the teachings of battle and magic and excelled at them all.

When God had given him the assignment to reign as the king of hell. Lucifer hadn't expected his mission in hell to last as long as it had. That resolute courage and will power had fortified him when he was forced to bestow punishment on the sinners. It had also proven to God it would be difficult to find any angel to replace him. It irritated God when Lucifer broke protocol and got bored and tried to test and tempt humanity, just to liven things up, but that was a small price to pay to have peace between him and Michael. It was also the means to the balance of good and evil.

Dante inherited his good looks from

Samael, as well as his lust for life. He excelled in criminal forensics and martial arts. He also inherited Samael silver's voice and loved to sing. He'd learned the art of magic from him and knew the rules of when to apply those powers. The combination of looks, charm and voice often got him into trouble, especially when it came to women.

Several decades ago, Samael went up to heaven and was having his annual dinner with his father and siblings on December 27th, when his father casually announced the birth of his first grandson. Everyone started asking questions all at once. Then they realized their father was looking directly at Michael and Samael. "Carolyn is a beautiful woman, isn't she, son?"

Both archangels flushed and had the decency to look down at the table.

Lailah laughed. "So, which one should I congratulate?"

God laughed. "Both of them. The boy

was fathered by both. And now they both get to make sure their progeny doesn't destroy everything they're supposed to protect."

That was half a lifetime ago. He'd long since grown used to the idea of having two fathers, and a horde of uncles and one aunt constantly watching over him.

It seemed along with his good looks and strength; he'd inherited a few other powers.

His fathers had forbidden Dante to use his powers unless there was no other choice. He could read minds, which had been useful when he was interrogating a suspect. Of course, his opinion of a life-or-death emergency and theirs often differed.

He could hear their words every day, "Son, you'll know when the time is right to administer justice, to help or torture someone if need be."

Not that it helped him in the break room the other night. He might as well have fought like hell instead of standing there and doing nothing. It wouldn't have changed the outcome of the fight, but it might've made his time in isolation easier.

Women had always been his weakness. His human half- brother had once told him. "Dante, you really need to stop using the old pullout system when you're screwing women.

You've got the potency of an army. Jeez, man, you've knocked that witch up twice already. I figured you'd learned your lesson by now. Number three is on the way and you're losing your freedom and your shield.

What the fuck is wrong with you? She's a witch and a fucking lunatic."

Dante smiled as he laid his face down against the cool tiles in his cell. He did that to see if the guards were coming near his cell. He loved his fathers, his brother and his sister. But the angel in his life was his mother, Carolyn. She was his heart and soul, the teacher of all that was good in the world. It was his mother that showed him what love truly meant. Her family and friends meant everything to her. She'd explained the truth of his birth and helped him to accept the reality of the archangels. She still loved them both equally.

He stood up and walked back to the narrow metal cot and noticed that Gus wasn't resting in his usual spot in his stained coffee cup. Then he heard a crunching sound in the far corner of the room. A large rat was standing on its hind legs. He was holding Gus and chewing his wings off. The rat's red eyes were glowing as it began to speak to Dante. "I know who you are boy and there's no escaping what's coming." "Oh really, who am I, rat boy? I'm guessing you're some lower-level demon that crawled out through a crack from hell. What is it that you want from me, demon?" "I'm just a messenger of the things to come. Your blood and soul will soon be the Duke of Hell's to devour." "I guess that's supposed to frighten me, huh, rat boy." Stop calling me rat boy you little monkey." "Reveal your name, you filthy scumbag. In the Lord's name, say your name and be gone." "We're the fallen ones and we're going to tear the souls out of every human being on earth. I'll start with your little friend here, Gus. He's very tasty. I'm the deadly Fur, Fur."

"Really that's one pathetic name. You're a fucking fur ball. Be gone, evil one." "You don't command me human."

The thin pad they gave him to sleep on wasn't thick enough to prevent the stainless steel from heating. The temperature outside was in the high nineties. Inside his cell it was damn well near a hundred degrees. He could feel the heat in the cell building and it was getting extremely hot.

He held his hand in the air and noticed a big difference in temperature. "Okay, pop, I know you're here. It's too damn hot inside this cell to be the weather. Come on out and say what needs to be said." It was at that moment the demon rat looked up from eating his meal and Dante heard a person snap his fingers and the rat exploded.

Samael appeared as his handsome, debonaire self. To Dante's surprise, his father, Michael also appeared. Neither looked especially happy to find their son in jail.

"To, what do I owe this pleasure? It's rare to have both of you show up at one time."

"Samael, I liked him better when he was a youngster. He wasn't such a snippy little shit."

"Brother, I must admit, you're absolutely correct. He got that mouth from you."

With that being said, the three of them laughed and hugged for several minutes. Samael's blood tears trickled down his cheeks and Michael's face glistened with a trail of holiness.

"Now that I have you here, would one of you explain why the fuck I'm in jail when I'm innocent of these crimes?"

Samael shifted uncomfortably, "Son, you know how much we love you, and want the best for you?"

"Yes, father I do, and I love you with all my heart and soul. But that doesn't explain why I'm here."

"Dante, it's all part of the plan. You know your grandfather doesn't like explaining himself. He expects us to do as he commands. That means you obey and don't ask questions.

We've charged you to act as God's shield between heaven and hell." Michael sighed. "Your grandfather considers you, his enforcer. He wants you here because something is going to happen and only you can prevent it. "

"Like what?"

"If we knew that we could have already taken care of it." Samael's voice went into a growl. He spoke as the king of hell would at a demon. "Dante Merrick, your job is to protect heaven and hell. When your time comes, you'll have the power to roam between both realms. But for now, you must stay in this cell and prepare yourself to stop whatever is about to happen. We suspect it has something to do with Allocén."

"Great". "Allocén is one of the Demon Dukes of Hell, except he was there before God assigned your father to bring some order down there. He's into the black art occult and commands the 36 legions of Hell's army. His demon soldiers will do anything for their commander. Some say he invented astronomy: others say it was a joke he pulled on humanity that got out of hand. Either way, he commands the Wiccan world. Whenever a witch seeks a familiar, she will invoke his name to call the familiar to her. Allocén has gathered a band of fallen angels on earth he calls the Watchers. There are rumors that the duke is convinced that a Nephilim's blood could wipe out humanity if used in the correct spell by a powerful witch. Of course, Allocén would have to destroy his soul first, and that's where the watchers come in. They're doing recon all over the world to locate the Nephilim. Dante, they're searching for you. They'll do anything for their leader, even if it means dying for him.

"So, what should I do?"

"Just do your time inside and build your mind and body. Study as much as possible on all the Fallen Ones and their ranks. We don't have enough time to teach you all of that right now. Then go to your three children and protect them from that evil harridan of a mother. It was your choice to sleep with her. We warned you, but you wouldn't listen. Now you must live with those decisions you've made. You'll have to teach the children about love and balance out the evil in her soul."

"Hopefully, the children will maintain enough of the good to become decent human beings."

Dante looked at both the archangels and asked. "Will they have angelic powers?"

"No, they don't have any of our powers." Michael took a deep breath and looked down at the floor. "Your grandfather granted you a few powers because he knew over the next few years misery and madness will fill the nations of Earth. You'll see glimpses of happiness, but don't be fooled by false trappings, because it makes you feel good. It's just a band-aid for the pain to come. The trials will shape you into a better man and archangel in the future. It may not help, that we've both been whispering in your ears, trying to teach you a balance between right or wrong. Lucifer tempts you on the dark side and I try to keep you pointed to the light. Make no mistake about this. Your father, Samael, pleaded with your grandfather asking to be released from the burden of Hell, so he could spend more time with you." Samael wept uncontrollably until his black wings were damp with blood tears.

Dante opened his arms and held his father as he spoke the words of the Lord. "Father. I'll never abandon thee and will always love you for all eternity. I know it's not in thy will or heart to do this to me. Let it be done to me, my fathers, and hear my prayers in my time of need. Please protect my children until I'm home with them. This is all I ask of you both. Be their shields against the evil that seeks them."

The two archangels' wings extended, and they took their angelic forms. They were enormous and intimidating. They looked down at their beloved son and spoke.

"We hear you, Dante Merrick, our beloved son. You'll face challenges from both heaven and hell. Hear our warning. The woman you fathered children with isn't from heaven or hell. She's a creature in a human skin suit, not an angel or demon. We don't know what she is, but we know she's not human. The oracles warn she will inflict physical and mental harm on your little ones once they reach an age where she can affect their development. For now, their innocence protects them, but as they age, the protection fades. We'll protect them at all costs. You must never leave your children like your mother's human husband left you and your siblings. Life is precious. Never forget that. Your human step-father, Ronaldo, is with your father Lucifer in hell, reliving his worst decisions he made while on earth."

"He's being tortured by a few Lucifer's warrior demons," Samael spoke quickly.

"Be strong and never leave the children's side. We're here for you and our family. We love your mother and our grandchildren. We are even fond of your half siblings, though they don't know what we are. You mustn't ever tell them of us. Carolyn swore she'd never divulge our identity. It won't be easy here, but it's important that you stay in jail. You'll know when the time is right. Goodbye for now, my son."

There was a brief whoosh of displaced air, and the cell was once again normal temperature. That was the last time he'd seen either of his fathers while he was incarcerated. The days became weeks, and the weeks had become months. His life had settled into a routine. Wake up, exercise, eat whatever they brought, exercise, sleep, wake up, read, exercise, eat whatever they brought, go back to sleep. He spent most of his time in isolation. Not by choice…once word got out, he was a rogue cop, everyone wanted a piece of him. It was easier to spend the time alone than in the clinic hospital. There had already been two attempts on his life there. The first time, the demons disrupted the cameras and put the clinic employees to sleep. This last time, one of the nurses was a watcher. It was all he could do to stay alive long enough to take her out. Luckily for Dante, her body disintegrated after he snapped her neck. The second nurse had found him on the floor, suffering from claw-like lacerations and frostbite. No one had an explanation for what happened, or any idea of where the missing nurse had gone.

***

Dante was sleeping deeply when his cell illuminated. Once his eyes had adjusted to the bright light, he saw the most beautiful being he'd could imagine. In his own way, the angel before him was as beautiful as his father.

"Awaken Dante, the time has come. Do not fear me, as I'm a messenger, from the all mighty high."

Dante sat up and swung his legs around to face him. "Yeah, I figured you worked for my grandfather."

He appeared surprised. "Do you know who I am?"

"Yes, you're my uncle, Gabriel. Only one angel is as handsome as my father, and you might even be better looking. Don't tell him I said that. Heard a lot of stories about you from both my fathers. Super brave.

Stunningly attractive. They also said you're an amazing musician and artist."

Gabriel's face broke into a smile that made his gut twinge. That was not a good feeling in a prison full of horny men. "Well, damn. Those two suck ups ruined my speech. You got me. At least I don't have to talk like it's still the thirteenth century. Now come over here and give your uncle Gabe a hug. I haven't seen you since you were still crawling on all fours."

They sat around and exchanged family gossip and a few tidbits of family history he'd never heard before. Most were about the other uncles and aunts neither father had thought to mention.

Finally, Gabe stood up and said, "the guards should be here soon. It won't be long before someone notices the camera is not working. It's time for me to put the mark upon your body. Remove your shirt, Dante. Wow, what are they feeding you, in here? You already have the physique of an Arch."

"Thanks, Uncle Gabe, I try to exercise as much as possible while I'm stuck here."

"Turn around, I need to examine your back. Damn, just as we suspected, your wings are budding. They're trying to break through the skin. It's the first sign that Armageddon is coming. We must move fast. I need to tattoo your back with a pair of Archangel wings. I made the ink from Archangel blood; it will appear as dark red angel wings to humans. The Arch blood won't be visible to them. Only the Arch's' can see it's true form. He paused and disappeared from sight.

Dante sighed and sat down on the bunk as the door opened and three guards entered the small cell. One kept his taser pointed at him as the other two tried to figure out why the camera wasn't working. After a few minutes, they left, taking the broken camera with them. Almost as soon as the door closed, Gabriel reappeared.

"I've filled the tattoo guns with Arch blood and maroon ink. It's going to take an hour or two to do the wings. Hope you don't mind sleeping on your stomach. Once the pain fades, I'll start on the rest of the tattoos."

"Wait, a minute. The rest?"

Yeah… another tiny detail your fathers left out. I need to tattoo the rest of your body in

Angelic writings and archaic sigils."

"Angelic writing? Why?"

"It not really writing, like you would write

a letter. It's actually pretty. Hang on and I'll show you." He stood and removed the long white tunic he was wearing. When he raised his wings; Dante could see the tattooed wings. He could also see a scattering of archaic sigils and runes tattooed around his back and sides. When he turned around, Dante could see the abjad glyphs continued on the front of his body The celestial script is our Lord's bible for exorcisms. You're to become heaven and hell's exorcist after the war is over."

He wasn't sure he was ready to fight the forces of hell any time soon. "They look old. What are they, Cyrillic?"

"Hebrew, Greek, a little Phoenician. A couple are so old, I don't even know where they came from. You could ask Samael, he's been around longer than any of us."

Gabriel was ready to begin the first session. He explained to Dante, "there will be eight sessions in total. Each session represents one Archangel that donated his blood. As the blood ink courses through your body, you'll adapt and become more powerful. Your grandfather hopes you will become the most powerful Arch of us all."

He removed a vial and shook a shimmery silver needle out and placed it in the tattoo gun. Gabe saw what he was looking at. "The needles are special. I cast them out of metal scrapings from our swords. Be still and don't move, it's not like I can start over. When I'm done, you'll no longer be just my nephew. You'll become my brother in arms." It took Gabriel two days to finish the meticulous artwork on Dante's body.

There were times Gabe thought Dante wouldn't survive the extricating pain. He'd never tried it on a half human. Then the ritual had to be performed over each sigil to activate it. When the last session was complete, Gabriel ran his hands over Dante's body and healed him instantly. "Look in the mirror, brother. You're now a walking exorcist bible." He saw the hesitation in Dante's eyes. "Don't worry. There aren't any markings on your face. We're not a South American drug gang."

"Very funny, Uncle Gabe." Dante looked at his back first and was in awe of the artwork Gabriel had done. "If you look close enough, you can see our blood running through the wings on your back. That's how we know you're the chosen one."

Dante felt a surge of energy throughout his body. He recited the words Gabe had taught him, along with the names of the symbols that decorated his body, starting with his father. "Saint Michael the Archangel, defend us in battle. Be our protection against the wickedness and snares of the devil. May God rebuke him, we humbly pray. And do thou, O Prince of the Heavenly Host, by the power of God, thrust into hell Satan and all evil spirits who wander through the world for the ruin of souls. Amen."

He looked at Gabriel but could read the message behind his expression. And started to recite the exorcism prayers.

"May I come to the assistance of the men and women God has created to his likeness and who he has redeemed at a great price from tyranny of evil. I'm your guardian and protector. The lord giveth me thy power to his entrusted souls and I'll lead them into heaven. I pray, therefore, the God of peace, to crush all the demons beneath our feet. I say your name and command you to leave this body and be gone. I cast you out, evil one. The power of our lord compels you."

After reciting the last verse on his body,

Dante collapsed into Gabriel's arms.

Gabriel laid him out on the metal bunk and covered him with the thin blanket.

Of all the archangels, he'd always had a soft spot for humanity. It had surprised him by how jealous he was when Michael and Samael conceived a half human child. Over the years, he'd watched Dante grow into a man and felt the pride a parent would have at his nephews' achievements. Now he watched over Dante's children, and worried if Dante would return in time. As a light flipped on in the hall outside the cell, he vanished.

PART - TWO

The correction officer knocked on Dante's cell door, waking him from a light doze. "Merrick, get up, your parole board hearing is in twenty minutes. Get cleaned up and be at the gate in ten minutes."

"Yes, sir, officer Halpin." He hated the idea of polishing the sadistic bastard's ego, but at this point, there was nothing he would do to ensure he got a good review today. Well… almost nothing. He had no idea how he'd fallen asleep. Last night he couldn't fall asleep no matter what he tried. Now he felt sluggish. He decided to do a few simple exercises to get his blood moving again.

Less than five minutes later, Dante finished the last set of pushups and put on his prison clothing. He vowed once he walked through those metal doors, he would wear no type of clothing that was orange. He still had a tremendous pump surging in his arms and chest from exertion, but even when his muscles relaxed, the material was still too tight. The nylon jumpsuit cut into his upper arms and his thighs, making it difficult to walk without ripping the seams. He took a deep breath and sat back down on the bunk, waiting to be escorted to the van that would transport him to the parole board building.

The actual trip passed in a warm blur. None of the inmates were in the mood to talk and that was fine with him. He was never especially sociable, and he was not willing to risk saying or doing anything that might ruin his chance of getting paroled. At least they took off the handcuff and ankle chains before they took him in.

Of course, the officer on duty at the door was someone he knew when he himself would escort one of his defendants there. He could see that the officer recognized him by the way he shifted his eyes away from his face, but at least he was respectful and pretended he did not know who he was.

"Inmate Merrick, please come inside and sit at the table across from us". The chairwoman of the board was in her late thirties, and a real looker. The other board members were three men that looked to be in their late 50s. He was curious about what she had done to rate the chair. None of the men looked like the type to enjoy having a woman lord over them.

It surprised him when she opened the questioning. "Mister Merrick, why are you here? We've all read your file. I even went to the extent of having the other 21 board members review your jacket. So, I asked you again. Why in the hell are you here?"

Dante sighed and explained the events that transpired the night in question. "Well, madam chairwoman, I was working a deep undercover assignment for the intelligence unit. I'd finally been able to get in with the Murphy boys who were in the organization known as The Westies. It's in the area known to you fine people as Hell's Kitchen in Manhattan. The geographical area covers from the South end of 34th Street to the North end of 59th Street. It covers from to the East River up to the

Hudson River. The Westies are a violent Irish gang, who work as muscle for the Italian Mafia. They're responsible for fifty percent of the mob's contracts. They're the hitmen for the five families in the five boroughs of NYC. I'd worked my way into the Murphy clan."

One man on the board interrupted Dante. "Excuse me, inmate Merrick, how in God's name did you infiltrate the Westies? You look very Italian to me."

"Yes, sir, my mother is Sicilian, and my fathers are a mix of everything."

"Fathers?"

"Oh, my mistake chairman, I meant father. I have enough family connections that I am very familiar with Irish traditions and history." "Thank you, please continue."

"The night in question, I was being initiated into the organization as a full member. Ian Doyle, The President of the Westies ordered me to carry out the execution of the Mob Capo Vincent Giancana, my best friend Tommy Giancana's father. They had caught him skimming off the top of their casino operation. So, the Don, Mario Colombo, ordered the hit and expected the Westies to handle it. Two other Westies from New Jersey accompanied me, seasoned hitmen whom I didn't know. I'd heard plenty of rumors about them, but none that could be substantiated. It didn't take long for me to realize I was being set up as a patsy. One of the sadistic Irishmen would execute me while the other took care of the mark. There was only one way they could've found out who I was. Someone inside the department informed them I was an undercover cop."

The chairwoman interrupted him. "Are you telling us your own people set you up?"

"Yes, that's correct Madam chairwoman."

"Please continue Dante." The other members looked over at her, as if to say, "why the hell are you calling this piece of crap by his first name?" He was curious, himself. After so many years inside, he had no delusions about his allure… orange nylon was an instant turn off.

She seemed to be interested in his responses. When he looked up in her direction, he'd noticed her blushing and squirming in her chair. He found that very amusing. When one of the board members frowned, he sighed and continued his story.

"We arrived at Vincent's home and were walking up to his house, when I heard the slide of an automatic weapon being released. The Westie that had introduced himself as Johnny Boyle, pressed a 45-automatic against my head and spoke, 'Time to die copper."' I spun around and clamped my hand around his silenced weapon and shoved it to the side as I grabbed the slide release, rendering it useless. Before he reacted, I sent a head butt into his face and shattered his nose and nasal cavity. The other hitman, Mickey Dwyer, shot me in the abdomen. As I was falling, I pulled my beretta from the small of my back and returned fire. I hit him three times, and one bullet killed him. Then I shot Johnny in his hand, making him drop his pistol. Lights were coming on inside the house, so I used a zip tie on Johnny and called for backup.

Vincent and his associates came rushing out of the house running down the driveway with their weapons out, ready to kill me. I looked up, and the Capo recognized me. He ordered his men to stand down and retreat back into the house. "Dante, what the hell is going on here, son?"

"They were going to execute you and your men, Uncle Vin."

"What was your role in this little plot, Dante?"

I pulled my detective shield out and told him, "I'm working undercover. You and your men must leave now. Get the hell out of New York and lie low for a few weeks. Go now and I'll take care of the rest." He grabbed my shoulders and kissed me on both sides of my cheeks and told me.

"Dante, you're one of the good ones. If you ever need anything, just reach out to the one of the family and they'll get word back to me. I have your six, son." He looked each board member in the eye, one by one. "Vincent had been a Marine for six years in Vietnam. He meant every word, and I knew it. When my backup finally arrived on the scene, two IAD lieutenants (internal investigation division accompanied them). They're the cops who investigate the street cops. It struck me as odd that IAD would respond so quickly to a sting operation that intelligence was conducting. You can imagine my surprise when they threw me to the ground and cuffed me."

He returned his eyes to the chairwoman. "My Intelligence Captain was screaming; "What the hell are you fools doing? He's one of us! Detective Merrick has been on a deep undercover assignment for the last eighteen months." One of the IAD bosses responded back saying,

"Well, he's being arrested on murder charges. You better get him a damn good lawyer. He's going to need one. We've been investigating him for two years. He's out of control."

"Out of control?"

"Our records show he has used excessive force on eighty percent of his cases." The red haired IAD boss, O Malley, was practically gloating as he watched me being placed in the back of his car.

"My captain yelled. "Yes, you moron, he goes after extremely violent criminals and at times must use force to apprehend and arrest them." "My captain's anguish was clear. He knew I was being railroaded but had no idea who was behind the push to get me off the streets."

"Six months later, I was stripped of my shield and tried for manslaughter. They acquitted me of that charge but found me guilty of Assault in the first degree, at the word of a repeat offender who was facing his third strike, and a life inside. The judge handed down a sentence of five years.

The state appointed attorney was a first-year graduate who'd never been in an actual trial. I ended up defending myself, after he got flustered and threw up in court. It was clear they would've murdered me if I hadn't taken action that night. I was in fear for my life and had no other option. It was self-defense. I've got to live with the fact that I took a man's life that night. For this I'm truly sorry for the victim and his family." "Thank you, for being honest with us, Dante. Do you have a permanent residence to live at if you're released?"

"Yes, I do. My mother owns an apartment and I have a room available there."

One of the other men asked, "It's evident you can't return to your prior employment. Do you have gainful employment waiting for you if you're out on the street?"

"Yes, I'll be working in the security field, sir. I've discussed this with the prison counsel and they've verified the position is waiting for me upon my release."

The man who asked began flipping through papers. Once he located the affidavit, he made a few notes and nodded.

They whispered amongst each other for a few moments, then the floor person spoke, "Thank you for speaking honestly with us today. You're excused, inmate, Merrick, and good luck to you in your future endeavors." She kept her face neutral and said nothing to indicate which way the vote might go. He tried to hide his disappointment but had expected no sign either way.

"Thank you, members of the board, for taking the time out of your busy day to listen to my plea to be released." Dante noticed the officer was now waiting behind my chair, so he nodded politely and made his way back to the holding area.

***

Dante nervously waited in his cell the next two days, praying to his grandfather, his fathers, and to all the Archangels. "Selaphiel, brother, if you can hear me. I beg you, to speak on my behalf to our lord, asking that he allow me to be set free. I can't take being looked at as a common criminal. You know I'm innocent of these crimes."

On the evening of the second day, the cell became illuminated with rays of light. Dante looked up and standing before him were two Archangels, who he'd never seen before. "I'm Jegudiel, brother. We know you've suffered by being wrongly imprisoned. It's your cross to bear alone, Dante. We can't interfere with free will and have to accept the human's decision."

"My name is Barachiel. You must accept this metaphorical cross, know the sorrows, and ask for our father's blessings, otherwise you'll have no salvation." Unlike the others, he never looked Dante in his eye. This made him wonder if they were contemplating if a half human was worthy of the Lord's blessings.

Dante stood before his brothers, and the tattoos on his body turned orange and glowed. He saw the doubt fade from Barachiel's eyes, but the dark-complexioned angel did not speak again. He simply faded away.

"I'll leave it in his hands and trust you all with my heart and soul." He wished he were more poetic with his words, but the archangel seemed to understand the meaning behind the simple words.

Jegudiel said goodbye and hugged him, then followed Barachiel back to heaven.

He stood there looking out the tiny window at the stars for some time after they'd left and wondered what would happen next.

***

A few days later, one of the Correction Officers slid a large yellow envelope under his cell door. His gut roiled, and his hands were trembling as he held the envelope in his hands. It surprised him how hard it was to open. Part of him wanted to rip it apart and the other part was afraid to read the words. Finally, he calmed his racing heart and read it. The letter said, Dante Merrick, has fulfilled the mandatory time for his sentence and is hereby paroled on October 1, 2013. It was as if it lifted a weight from his chest. Free! He looked at the calendar on the wall and counted the days he had left in that hellhole.

"Twenty-one days until I get home to my kids. I can make it through this, standing on my head," he spoke the words out loud, as if it would only be true if he heard them. Or so he thought. The cake walk he'd imagined was no picnic at all.

As if someone had painted a large target on his back, he'd become the target of every lifer inside the prison. The other inmates tested him more now than ever before. Over the next few weeks, he'd been stabbed and suffered several broken ribs. They transferred three especially large inmates to his cell block under some very sketchy circumstances. No one was certain who they were, but everyone said their jacket listed them as lifers. Nor had anyone been given any advanced notice. Within a week of the day after he received the letter, three older lifers died, and the guards moved them in. They ruled the deaths natural, as all the men were over sixty and in poor health, but it was unusual to move someone into their vacant beds the same day. The three appeared to know each other, even though their papers listed them as transfers from different facilities.

Dante was an expert in the fighting arts and in tremendous shape since there was little to do except exercise inside. The first attack happened exactly as prison stories warned while he was taking a shower. The unknown man had wrapped soap inside a wet towel and used the makeshift weapon as a bludgeon, striking his body repeatedly. The attack by the new inmate surprised him. Dante was expecting him to be strong, since his size and physique were like his own, but this man had the strength of ten. Each blow was stronger than the previous one. He felt the first rib crack, but after that he was too busy concentrating on staying alive.

He heard a voice call out, "Enough! The guards are coming."

The new man left abruptly, leaving him leaning against the wall.

Several days later, two more engaged him in a fight.

That attack, they came together. One bumped him in the yard and drove a kitchen knife he'd stolen from the mess hall into Dante's side. The second distracted the guard. He had cut his hand while gripping the knife to prevent it from going in more than once. That was most likely what saved him. It was long enough to severely damage his kidney. The guards saw nothing. It was only after one of the other inmates saw the blood and pointed to him that anyone realized he'd been stabbed.

The third attack was the worst. You would think he'd be safe inside the prison clinic, but that was a joke. Somehow, the two men had become three. The faculty had brought them in to be monitored by the staff because of their erratic behavior. There was only one other patient in the ward beside him. One nurse was on duty, a sweet older woman who was married to one of the maintenance supervisors.

All three men displayed perfect manners while being moved to the clinic. They reacted sluggishly when the nurse took their vitals and gave them something to make them sleep. They were all on the other end of the clinic and kept in isolation in case whatever was affecting them was virulent.

Something about their behavior had Dante on edge. There was no way he was going to fall asleep with them in the same unit. His intuitive consciousness was clamoring alarms. Even the other patient was shifting uncomfortably in his sleep. When the attack happened, it took everyone by surprise.

The nurse stopped at the first inmate to check his vitals and adjust the drip. He suddenly reached up, clamping his hands around her throat, moving faster than any human should be able to move. The sharp snap of her neck breaking echoed in the silence of the clinic. Dante could have heard it break without his enhanced hearing.

By the time her body hit the floor, all three were on their feet and moving his way.

Dante had seen men act similarly when they were jacked up on the hallucinogenic drug PCP. The metabolism was surging, their strength and speed increased beyond normal human boundaries. Several years earlier, he had done an undercover investigation on a MC (Motorcycle club) that was dealing and manufacturing the illegal narcotic. Angel dust was an extremely dangerous anesthetic that induced hallucinogenic episodes in humans when taken. Anyone taking the drug exhibited trance like behavior, and increased violent tendencies, often to the point where once locked in, nothing could distract them from their target. It was like a fucking time bomb exploded. The drug made average men into wrecking crews; the three giants heading his way could rip the average human limbs from his body.

He'd rendered one man semiconscious during the shower altercations, but it took every ounce of his human strength and training he had in him to do so. His grandfather had forbidden him to use his angelic powers while incarcerated. It was going to take a miracle to survive this attack. He started talking to God, hoping to at least have a fighting chance. "Well, Grandpa, I could really use one of your miracles right now. I've lived by your rules. But I get the feeling these guys are playing for the other team. I could use some divine interference right now."

When no archangel appeared to help him, he pulled the needle from his arm, picked up a bedpan and prepared to go down fighting. He noted that the older man in the other bed was moving toward the open office door. The deadly trio hadn't noticed, and Dante didn't want to do anything to draw their attention to his escape.

As the first of the men reached for him, he swung the bed pan, hitting him upside the head. The blow would have dropped a bull. He barely flinched. Damn.

There was nothing Dante could do to hurt him, the first man reached for his arm, wrapping his fingers and hand around Dante's wrist, he squeezed. Dante was staggered by the pain as two of his carpal bones snapped. The second man was reaching for him as the third made his way behind him, intending to come in on his unprotected side. As the final two touched his body, Dante's tattoos began glowing. First, he noticed that the men no longer looked human; it was as if someone had overlaid a human body atop the twisted, overly muscled shape of a demon. He caught glimpses of withered flesh, horns, fur, and scales as the image continued to writhe and twist beneath the light from the glowing glyphs. It became a race to see who would fall first, Dante or the demons. One had slipped his arm around Dante's neck, and he was finding it harder to breathe. Just as he was certain he was about to die, he heard bullets striking the bodies of the three demons. The last thing he remembered was thinking, It's about time.

***

There was nothing that sounded better than the gates closing behind him. Five days later, he was out of that hellhole. There was never a possibility of him ever going back. His mother was waiting at the gate along with the Captain from the Intelligence unit. As he expected, there was no sign of his wife and children.

"How are you, son?" his mother asked as she put her arms around him for the first time in five years.

"I'm fine mother, I'm just glad this is over. Now I can move on with my life."

Captain Blackman shifted uncomfortably, looking much older than he had when Dante was incarcerated. "You have no idea how glad I am to see you walk free. Call this man once you get settled in at home. You'll be working under his umbrella as an investigator."

"Thank you, boss, for all that you've done for me. It was good to know you had my back when everyone else turned away."

Captain Blackman shook his hand and headed back to begin his shift. The captain turned and said, "Things aren't the same around the station as they were when you were a part of the unit. Good luck detective. You'll always be a detective in my book and the best I've ever had. Godspeed Dante." He nodded to Blackman as he walked away.

"Hungry? I am, let's get some breakfast before we start back. I'm sure you can eat after all that prison food." One thing hadn't changed. His mother still wanted to feed him at every opportunity.

Dante only wanted to get as far away from the prison as possible. In the back of his mind, he could hear imaginary voices saying, "We've made a mistake. You have to come back inside." Once they were in the car and moving, it began to sink in that he really was free.

He ate a large breakfast, enjoying a ribeye, three eggs over medium, and fried potatoes scattered all over the plate, and some of the best coffee he could remember. Afterward, the ride back home to Brooklyn, New York, seemed to fly by.

"Mom, instead of going straight home, take me by to see the kids."

"Are you sure you want to do that? It's been five years. They may not remember you." Her voice quivered, so Dante could tell she was worried.

"Yeah. Take me there." He leaned back in the seat, praying that he hadn't made a mistake.

Several hours after walking out of the prison, Dante knocked on the door of his home. His three children answered the door. My goodness, how the children had grown. They not only recognized him; they were also elated to see him. He gathered them into his arms, enjoying their scent and the way they felt after so long. Their voices were unfamiliar, and they were taller. He had to admit, hugging the youngest was strange. It was the first time he'd seen his youngest son since he was a baby.

The sneer on their mother's face gave an entirely different message. His wife stood behind them as he got reacquainted. Once she was certain he'd greeted all the children, she said, "Welcome home. I'm heading out. Can you watch the kids for the next two days?"

"Sure, I can. I've got a question. What would've you done had I not shown up today? Who was going to watch my kids?"

"I had Justine, from down the street, coming over to babysit them for the next three days."

"Unreal, she's what… fourteen years old? She probably can't even take care of herself, and you were going to leave them with her for two days?"

"Hey, listen, convict, I've been dealing with them for the past five years. I need a fucking break. So, fuck you and the convict train you rode in on. Do you want me to call your parole officer and say you threatened me? Your ass will be back in prison before you've sat down."

He rolled his eyes and gave up. She would lie through her teeth if she thought it would benefit her. "Have a nice time, Mara."

"I, will, you fucking dickhead."

It was only after she pulled away; he realized he didn't know where she was going or who she was going with. It was October 30th, so he had his guesses, but a lot could've changed since he went to jail. Either way, she was home on the first, in time to pick up her monthly check, and He finally moved into his mother's spare room.

***

The year went by quickly and the kids adapted to having their loving father back in their lives. They could feel and sense that he was their protector from the evil shrew that they called their mother. Somehow, over the five years, she'd changed from a bossy hellcat into a bullying old battle axe. It was a festering coil of evil he could see writhing in her soul. One day he had to work late observing a cheating husband. Mara had been on a tear all day, screaming and cursing at the kids. One of them had broken a figurine and hid it in the broom closet. Mara found it when she was taking out the vacuum.

"Get the hell down here, all of you, right now. Stand in the squares in front of you. If any of your feet move outside the square, I'll chop your foot off. Who broke my mother's Elsa figurine?" She screamed in each child's ear. "Who, broke it? Tell me and you won't get punished." She knew she couldn't leave any marks on the children's faces. Dante would notice it and he might alert the authorities. None of them said a word and remained silent. Even though it was fall, it had been a hot September day, and the kids were wearing shorts to keep cool.

"Who broke the figurine?

The children were resilient and stayed silent. "Okay, you little wiseasses. She went to the food pantry and grabbed a five-pound bag of raw rice and poured it on the floor in front of their feet. "Kneel on the rice and don't move until one of you admits their sin."

After two hours of watching them cry and telling her that the rice was hurting their knees, she finally tired of them interrupting her shows. During a commercial break for the soap opera, General Hospital, she got up off the sofa and walked over to the kneeling children. She ordered the youngest, "get up and go to your room and don't come out. You can only leave to go to the bathroom. Is that understood, mister man?"

"Yes, mother." He wasted no time before running toward the stairs.

"As for you two little shits, keep kneeling and stop your sniveling."

Just then Mara's phone rang. She gazed at the kitchen clock. It was 4:00 pm, It was Dante. "I'm ten minutes out. Do you need anything?"

"No, I don't. Why are you getting back so early? What did you do, get fired or arrested again?"

"You're a barrel of laughs, Mara. No, I closed out the investigation I was on and thought I would spend some time with the kids."

"Good, I've got plans tonight with some people from work and will be gone all night."

He sighed. He'd long since given up on the possibility of them ever becoming a couple again. "That's fine. Where are the kids?"

"They're upstairs watching a movie." She hung up without another word.

Something was wrong. He could sense his children were in danger. He needed to get there as fast as possible. He whipped onto the freeway and raced toward the house, praying that their innocence would protect them and they'd be safe when he arrived.

"You, two have been punished long enough. Get up and clean the floor and throw out the rice. Don't break anything else in the house. Not a word about this better get to your father. Got it? Are we clear on that?"

"Yes, mother, we won't tell pops."

"Tell, your brother to come downstairs. I'll order some pizza for dinner."

"Yes, Ma'am." The two older children raced to clean up the bloody rice before their father arrived.

Ten minutes later, Dante rushed into the house. Mara was ready to leave as soon as he walked through the door. She never mentioned the name of the friend she intended to meet, and he never asked. In the back of his mind, he wondered if the friend was also her lover. The woman loved sex, so he was certain she was seeing someone.

The self-satisfied smirk on her face gave him chills.

"Have a nice night, don't stay up for me."

"I never do, Mara."

She slammed the door and was gone.

Dante looked into the eyes of his children and could see the fear in them. "What happened today? What did she do to you kids? Did she hurt any of you?"

"No daddy, we promise everything is fine. We played outside all day and had fun." The oldest child could not hide the fear in her eyes.

What had she done to his children?

Dante felt the rage coursing throughout his body. His wings were protruding, the upper curve stretching the material to the point of breaking through his t-shirt.

His daughter noticed it and said, "Pops, what's happening to your back, it's getting swollen?"

"Nothing honey, I'm probably allergic to something I ate earlier. Don't worry, pumpkin, everything is okay."

He pulled off his tee shirt and looked in the mirror and could see it was far being normal. His angelic senses were sending signals that something horrible was about to befall humanity.

"Dad, your angel wings are so cool. It looks like blood going through tubes."

"What did you say, son?"

"It looks like blood running through a tube. Like when you go to the doctor and the nurse takes your blood."

"Okay, you three rug-rats go get cleaned up and brush your teeth and hit the sac. I'll tuck you in when you're finished and in your PJs. I'm taking you to, Great Adventure tomorrow. Just the four of us. Your mother has work."

"Yay, we're going to have so much fun on the rides. Love you dad."

"I love you kids more than you'll ever know."

When the children had finally fallen asleep, Dante called to his fathers. "I need to speak with both of you, right now."

Michael appeared first. "What is it, son?"

Dante spoke angrily, "Let's, wait for the king of hell to get here."

The room grew hotter at that very moment. "He'll be here any second now." Michael said, as plumes of smoke swirled along the living room floor.

"Well, howdy partners, how goes it up here?"

"Father, we don't have time for your shenanigans. We've got a real problem. First, my wings were aching to come out tonight while I was having dinner with the kids. I sense they'd been harmed, but they all swore nothing had happened to them. I'm sure they were lying to me, to protect Mara."

"Dante, have you ever considered, it was out of fear of that evil harridan they call their mother?" asked Michael. "Of course, I have, father. That's not the worst of it. I thought Gabriel had told me that only Archangels could see the Arch's blood running through my tattooed wings."

"That's correct son, we're the only ones that can see it." Samael looked puzzled.

"You, both told me that the kids don't possess any angelic powers, correct? Well, here's a human news flash. All three children could see the blood moving throughout the winged tattoo. In fact, they were giggling about how they loved looking at all the artwork on my body, especially the angel wings on my back. They love how the wings looked, as if the red lines were running through the artwork."

"Well, I'll be a monkey's uncle." "No Samael, we're three monkey's grandfathers." Both the angels started laughing hysterically.

"Are you quite finished with the stupid human jokes? Did you forget, the woman of your dreams, and son are human?"

Samael stood up and vocalized, "Watch your tone with us. We're just having some fun with each other. We rarely get the time to do that anymore."

"I apologize father for my outburst."

"What else could we expect, your half human."

"Hilarious, Father Michael."

Michael placed his hands on Dante's shoulders and told him to remove his shirt.

After Dante removed the white tee shirt he was wearing., he examined his son's back. "Shit, Armageddon will be upon us in the next few days."

"Wait a minute. First, you don't know why my children can see the glyphs and sigils glowing and archangel blood running through the wings on my back. And now you saying Armageddon is about to happen?"

His father shrugged. "It's possible that any scion could see the markings. I know you were told no one could see it, but to be honest, no one really knows. You're unique.

And your children are unique."

Samael was still studying the wings and the angelic symbols of his brother's inscriptions. They were turning brighter orange as both archangels read them. "The time is coming Dante, when you'll have to become heaven and hell's protector. This burden can't be lifted from your soul. It's your cross to bear." As Samael was telling him that, he began to tear up. "I'm sorry, son, that you've got to go through this alone.

Allocén has escaped Hell and is roaming the earth searching for Moses' staff. I've consulted with all the other Arch's and we're preparing for the war that's coming."

"Will you take the side of the fallen ones in hell, father?"

"No, Dante, I'll crush any of them who try to hurt you, or my brothers. I'm the bearer of light, and I have Azazel's flaming sword with me to fight on the side of heaven and humanity. Only the rumors spread by the demons made anyone believe I was evil."

Dante asked, "what does Moses' staff have to do with all of this?"

Michael sat down before he revealed the powers the staff held. "When our father told Moses to free his people, he gave him powers through the staff. He used it to free the Israelites and spread the word of the father almighty. But there was a fallen angel with great powers present when Moses led his people into Israel. His name was Purah. The almighty named him the Conjurer of the Dead and Seeker of Hidden Secrets. He uncovered the secret crypt where Moses had the staff and stole it. He then inscribed a powerful sigil into the staff which restores life after death."

"He could bring the dead back to life." "Like The Walking Dead show?"

"No, not like television zombies. It resurrects any human or demon back to their normal life. Whether they were evil or good it does not matter. Allocén was angry when our father sentenced his brother Purah to death for treason against heaven for using black magic on the artifact."

Michael nodded solemnly. "Raphael and I had to carry out his death sentence. Allocén swore revenge on us and swore to bring down our family. For that we threw him into hell and he became a fallen one."

"So, he wants his brother back alive?"

"Not just that. God created the staff to part the sea for Moses. It can open any pathway. With the staff, Allocén can open a portal between hell and earth and bring forth his armies."

"Just for the record," Samael said, "Vampires are real and have existed for thousands of years. You'll be fighting plenty of them in the future. Quite a few demons, too. We'll tell you the history about the Vampires when the time comes. It quite a story in itself. There are several that protect humanity and punish evil humans and at times, evil Vamps." He hesitated, and Michael urged him to continue. "Michael and I have discovered a few things about your children's mother. She's a direct descendent of the first female angel, Lilith. The humans removed most of the references to her when they wrote the bible. Lilith searches for children to kidnap and kill them, and your children would be perfect for her plans." "I thought Lilith was the first human?" "No, that was Eve. The apostles got that right. Lilith was my partner." Samael somehow managed to look sheepish. "I know. I screwed that up on my own. Dante, you'll have to trap Mara and bind her with the Everlasting Chains. Then send her into the place known as the darkness for eternity. That's where all the fallen angels who've become demons are sent when they're repeat offenders against our father laws." Michael nodded. "It's a 'pocket dimension', a small one, but it's perfect for a prison. Samael and I have been placing angelic offenders there for eons. Only a few other Arch's know that we're the Justice Keepers for your grandfather. It's a hard secret to keep. We've never revealed our true identities to the captured ones. We administer justice unto the offender and banish them into the darkness."

"Now it's time for you to become the third and final Justice Keeper."

"That's all fine and dandy. I'll do whatever I'm told to do. But tell me the answer to why my children, your grandchildren, can see the angelic blood ink moving throughout the angel wing tattoo."

"I'm guessing as they're maturing, the angelic half of them is revealing itself. Remember, they've got Lilith's bloodline in them as well. It seems like our Arch blood is stronger than Lilith's demonic contribution. So far, anyway. If you think they are stubborn now, imagine if they shifted from good to evil?"

"Let's just pray that they don't fall and become demons." Samael took his Lucifer form again and growled. "I'll lay my life and soul down for them. I can't allow that to happen to our grandchildren."

"Easy brother, take it easy, neither will I. We're the children's protectors, as well as Carolyn's." At that moment, Michael looked even more dangerous than when his brother had taken the form of lucifer. Samael tried shifted back into his angel human form.

"Okay. let's sit down so we can discuss our options and plan out how to locate and chain Allocén." Dante waived them toward the kitchen table. "There's pizza in the box if you're hungry."

Samael reached for a plate and the box. Then he asked Dante, "do you have any holy water? I'm dying of thirst?"

"Won't that burn your insides up, father?" "My lord, did you watch that silly movie again. What is it? The Exorcist?"

"Sorry father, I was just worried that it would harm you. Regular water won't work?"

"No, when he gets like this, he needs holy water."

"I don't have any in the house. I can run down to the church on the corner and ask a priest to bless some."

Michael laughed. "Dante, you're the Exorcist Priest of Heaven and Hell. just bless the water with the words written on your left arm."

Dante blushed. It had never occurred to him that his fathers might consider him a priest. He picked up a bottle of filtered water and spoke the words on his arm. The words were a combination of the angelic language combined with a few old-fashioned words of Latin. "Bless this water and the hand of the cup of our father." The bottle took on a faint glow for a few seconds.

Dante smiled and then handed Samael the bottle.

His father guzzled it down and turned back to his human form.

Michael and Samael were both beaming with pride.

"Brother, he's passed the ultimate test," Michael announced with a joyful voice. Samael grabbed his son, beaming with fatherly pride. "That's our boy, Michael, that's our boy. Your mother would be so proud if she were here."

There was a soft laugh from the doorway. "But I am Samael. Gabriel came and picked me up so I could witness the glorious event that's just taken place. Now we can celebrate with our son."

Gabriel looked almost as happy as his brothers. Everyone was hugging and smiling and talking at one time.

Dante heard the soft sound of little footsteps coming down the stairs and motioned for the others to be quiet. It was too late. The inquisitive child had already noticed them. The boys were right behind her on the stairs.

"Pops, who are all these people in our living room?" His daughter was watching them as they shuffled and settled down in the armchairs and sofa.

"These are your grandfathers Michael, Samael and Uncle Gabe. You already know grandma.

You might as well come down and meet them."

The archangels held out their arms to hug the little ones. After a few minutes of smothering them with hugs, they kissed them goodnight. Then Gabriel touched each of the children's foreheads and whispered. "Forget what thy have seen here tonight." Upon his touch, each child fell back asleep.

For the rest of the evening, the happy archangels let one precious child sleep on their lap. Finally, Gabriel said his goodbyes and carried the youngest boy up to his bed before returning to his duties in heaven.

Michael and Samael sat on either side of Carolyn and held her hands as they discussed a battle plan to capture Allocén. They'd often called Mara a witch, but now they realized she was literally one. Because of this, they couldn't banish her into the darkness. It would have to be Dante.

"We must find the staff before Allocén or one of his agents locates it. If it gets into his hands, only our father knows what hell he'll unleash on humanity. We've got to stop him at any cost."

Samael wasn't sure what his pious brother was thinking through what he said., but he was. "I agree brother, at any cost."

Dante did not remember falling asleep on the sofa, but someone had covered him with a thick blanket and removed his shoes. He wasn't sure if it was the morning sunlight or the children that woke him. By the time he took a shower and dressed, the children had already eaten breakfast and were ready for the day. Their excitement was easy to see. They were practically dancing from anticipation of their day at the amusement park. The two youngest were holding hands and singing, "we're going to, Great Adventure today with daddy," over and over.

It turned out to be a wonderful day for all of them. Michael, Samael, Raphael, and Gabriel snuck into the park and disguised themselves as tourists. They rode the rides with their niece nephew, and grandchildren. Night finally came, and they were so tired no one complained when Dante called it a day and said it was time to head back home.

"Did you kids have fun today?"

"We sure did. Daddy. Thank you for taking us," his oldest son said.

His fathers and uncles were flying, and riding on top of the roof and called down to the inside, "We had fun too, son. Thanks for taking us along."

Dante whispered, "you're welcome."

PART - THREE

One month later, Dante had learned the hard way that being on the side of good wasn't always the easiest path to follow. His father Michael, started to explain what they were truly up against.

"What makes these three any worse than the others?"

Michael thought for a moment. "Allocén has begun to show his power by bringing forth two of his two most faithful soldiers to help him in locating the staff." The demonic pair would prove to be some of the toughest Watchers that Dante would ever need to send into the darkness.

"Well, son, these are not the typical demon soldiers you've faced since ascending. Dantanian, a fallen angel who we call 'the Shifter', can shift his appearance and disguise himself as anyone, including an ally archangel. As if that isn't enough to deal with, he can also read people's thoughts, just like Samael can. He doesn't possess the ability that Samael has, not even close. But he's still dangerous. One thing he likes to do is take control of a human mind, making them do

things they wouldn't normally do. I know you've been trained in reading people's minds, but you haven't perfected it like Samael has. You must keep training with him in the art of reading one's mind.

"Could Dantanian read my mind?"

"Who knows? Until you've face him, there's no way to know what might happen. There's never been anyone like you. One thing you must do is train your mind and perfect reading demons and angels minds. You're already excellent at reading the human mind. We'll help you with that in the coming days."

"So, what about the other one, …Asmodeus?"

"He's one of the evilest of the fallen angels. He's the Lords of witches and earned the rank of an Archdemon in Hell."

"I seem to remember reading something about him. Wasn't he one of the most beautiful angels? The one that fell from grace after falling in love with a beautiful human named Sarah?"

"Yes, that's correct. That lust drove him to kill seven prospective husbands to keep her pure and untouched. Finally, Raphael bound him in Hell after damaging his leg with the demon's own War Hammer. The leg healed incorrectly, and he now walks with a limp."

"That has to suck. So, he has a constant reminder of how much he hates Raphael."

"I imagine it is. But make no mistake of thinking that will make him any less dangerous. Both archangels are cunning and extremely powerful. They'll use their God given strength in their efforts to destroy humanity. As a Watcher they've sworn a blood oath to wreak havoc on earth and will stop at nothing to accomplish their mission."

"So, what do we do now?"

"We have reason to believe that the Watchers are concentrating their search in the Atacama Desert in Chile. No one lives there, and it's such a desolate place, even the animals avoid it. That's why Raphael hid the staff there."

"So, there's a chance the Watchers might find the staff?"

"Unless we find a way to stop them, there's a very good chance they will."

***

Asmodeus picked up a handful of sand and held it under his nose. "We're close, my lord. I can smell the ancient Kauri wood the staff is made of. That staff is over 3600 years old. It's amazing that it's still in one piece."

"You'd think the All High would've chosen a more common species. Good work. How far are we from it, Asmodeus?"

"I'd say, roughly two kilometers, from where the archaeologist claimed it was buried. I'm sure we can find the red cavern soon. After that, it should be simple to locate the staff."

"There's a lot of red caverns here, Asmodeus. Time is of the essence; I need that staff before the blood moon rises tomorrow night," Allocén roared.

Asmodeus placed his hand against his forehead to shield the sun from his eyes. After a century in the bowels of Hell, the bright light bothered his eyes, making his vision blur. He slowly did a full 360 and said, "the wood scent is that way. If we hurry, we can reach it before nightfall."

"That's too long. There are no humans around to see you, so fly there. I want the staff in my hands before the sun is high overhead." The bright sun bothered his eyes, but he would never display the slightest weakness before the other demons. Now that the End of Time was near, he had to force himself to remain calm and think. The urge to spill blood was overwhelming.

"Allocén, I need a drink. I'm thirsty," Dantanian whined.

"Take your drink and stop being a little bitch. Since we're going to fly, we no longer need a driver."

The driver's eyes opened wider at Allocén's words. He fumbled for the jeep's keys. Just as he pushed the brass key into the ignition, he felt Dantanian hand clamp down on his shoulder. He didn't have time to scream before the demon snapped his neck.

***

Mara took a long drag off her cigarette and exhaled it through her nostrils. She smiled and thought to herself. "That's right, you little bastards, I'm the dragon lady and soon you're all going to die in flames." She was giving the death stare to her three children and Dante. They were playing 'tag you're not it' in the backyard.

Her daughter looked over at her and froze like a deer in headlights. The little girl kept saying to herself, "mommy's a witch, she's a witch."

Mara's eyes grew cold and black at her words. How did the child know?

Her daughter thought, "I can't tell daddy she hurts us and is always yelling. He'll get angry with her and might hurt her. Then he'll go back to jail, and we'll be all alone with her." The little girl turned around as quickly as she could and jumped onto Dante's back. "Give me a piggyback ride, daddy."

All the kids pile on top of him. One by one, they got rides from their father.

Mara watched for a few moments and then went back into the house. It wouldn't be long now before the children were no longer protected by their innocence.

Later that evening, Mara yelled up to Dante, who was reading a bedtime story to the kids. "I'm leaving for the next three days with friends. We're going to Massachusetts to visit Salem."

"That's fine, I'm off from work. See you when you get back." Under his breath Dante muttered, "With any luck they'll burn you at the stake."

The door slammed shut behind her and he raced down the stairs to see who was in the car with her.

The outer form was of a middle-aged man, but he could see the demon beneath the human overlay. His head turned toward the house and Dante could see the red flashes in his vermillion eyes. "That's no human, he's a fallen one for sure." This unnerved Dante for a few seconds but he soon gathered his emotions. Just before the car pulled away, he heard a voice in his head speaking only to him. "You're the one that's destined to save humanity? The Nephilim that's called to be the third Justice keeper? Have you read through all the rites of exorcism, Priest? You're going to need them, for what's coming to earth." Then the car pulled away.

Dante reached for a set of prayer beads his mother had given him and commanded the spirit, "show yourself and reveal your name demon. I know you're no arch. Reveal to me your identity now. I command thee in the name of Christ the Almighty son of heaven and the holy father."

He heard distant laughter. "My army comprises hundreds of the fallen ones. Tell me, who am I, half-breed?"

Dante knew there were only a few with enough power to rule over that many watchers. "You're Semyaza, the leader of demons called the Watchers of Hell."

"Very good, little priest. You can be rest assured we shall meet in person one day soon.

For now, I'll take my enjoyment from your wife." The laughter continued but faded as the car moved further away from the house.

Dante tore his shirt off and placed his palm over his chest and recited the angelic sigils of the archangels. "I call upon my brothers; Michael, Gabriel, Raphael, Uriel, and Samael, to protect this house and thy children from the abomination Semyaza, and his horde of demon soldiers." Seconds later, a fallen angel named Buniel appeared in the living room.

The room, illuminated with fires from hell and a bright light of heaven. The demon took his demonic form as a dragon with three heads. Dante held his hand in the air and yelled out the command. "Chains of justice." The everlasting chains appeared and wrapped around his hand and forearm. He then extended his arm and used the chains as a bullwhip. The chain caught the demon and the links coiled around Buniel's neck and wrapped around his arms and legs. Dante spoke the words of imprisonment and vanquished the demon into the darkness. But his black soul twirled around the room and headed towards the stairs where the children were sleeping. Dante whipped the chains at the black smoke and destroyed his soul, then he inhaled the demon's grace.

A few seconds later, the room returned to its normal look and was again peaceful. It was only later he wondered if Mara had heard his conversation with Semyaza.

***

Samael and Michael were silent as they listened to Dante's story. His fathers were in awe of how Dante had used the chains as a whip. Despite years of practice, none of the archangels had mastered that maneuver. Only the All High had performed that impossible move, and that was many, many eons ago.

Michael questioned his son, "how and where did you learn to do that?"

"Yeah, no archangel has ever been able to duplicate that move. We all kept getting smashed in the head when we tried it. Who showed you how to do it? Have you been training without us?" Samael was both proud of Dante and envious at the same time.

"No one trained me or showed me how to use the chains. It just happened. Buniel appeared in the living room and I extended my arm in the air like I'd been doing it for years and yelled chains of justice. The chains came down and wrapped around my forearm and hand. I just snapped my arm like a bullwhip in his direction and the chains coiled around him and I went to send him into the darkness, but his soul tried to escape and I hit it with the chains, and it disintegrated into thin air. I captured his remaining grace and consumed it."

"Well, Samael, you might as well give him his gift now. We'll talk more about your grace eating another time." The gift was a wooden hand-crafted chest with an ancient lock on it. "The combination is your mother's birthday, 21748."

"Do you like it?" Michael asked. "It's made from the same wood as Moses's staff."

"It's beautiful! Did you make it?" Dante was really pleased with his gift.

"No, Joseph made it."

"Joseph, Jesus' father made the box?"

Samael smiled, showing the briefest glimpse of pointed canines. "Yes, his birth father. He was a splendid craftsman. He even made the throne I sit on in hell. You know, old Lucifer's house. You can check in, but you can't check out."

The three of them started to laugh hysterically. "He also made the dining room set we use during our celebrations in heaven. It's much nicer than they show in the painting of the last supper." Michael turned to his brother. "Samael, why didn't his wings extend during the altercation with Buniel?"

"I assume it's still not time for him to fully embrace his angelic powers. Remember what we told him? He'll know when the time is right, and it will just happen. I just hope we're there when it does."

***

Allocén and his two soldiers reached the red cavern after noon. Asmodeus was certain they'd hid the staff somewhere inside. The scent trail had grown stronger as they approached the area. They circled the location

twice before landing, to ensure there were no hidden dangers. They expected that the path to the staff would be littered with unseen traps, each designed with demons in mind. They assumed the Archangel believed the staff was hidden so well it could never be discovered. If he'd know that a human or fallen one could find it. He would've taken further precautionary steps to ensure its safety.

They crept through the dark underground chambers, enjoying the cooler temperatures and murky ebon shadows after days of searching under the bright sun. Asmodeus held a glowing globe in his hand that would alert him when they'd reached the general section where the artifact had been hidden.

"The needle is moving, my lord." He held up the globe so Allocén could see the needle floating inside.

"Which way now?" Dantanian inquired. "Stay to your left, we're almost there. A few more steps and we should be close."

"I see nothing that would indicate anything had ever been hidden here."

"Did you think he would leave a sign saying, 'dig here for staff?" Dantanian snapped back to Asmodeus.

Allocén shouted to them. "Start wasting my time. If it's time to dig, then start digging and don't stop until we have that staff in my hands."

Asmodeus jokingly asked, "do we get a dinner break and a 15-minute coffee break. After all, we're in the Watcher's union."

Dantanian laughed uncontrollably at his brother's words.

Allocén glided over to them, lifting both demons off the ground by their necks and squeezed until both were struggling to breathe. "Do I look like I'm here on vacation? I'll snap your fucking necks and, eat your souls, if you fuck this up. Do I make myself clear?"

"Yes, my lord, sorry."

Several hours later, they were still digging and found nothing. Both demons worried they wouldn't find the staff and subsequently be killed by their leader. Finally, frustrated with the entire search, Dantanian decided he needed a break. He shoved his shovel down into the red clay, intending to start digging in a different area when he returned. The sound of metal ringing off stone made him hesitate. He grabbed the shovel and began frantically digging. Less than a foot down, he struck a long rectangular shaped stone. "I think I found something!"

All three demons jumped into the pit and clawed the sand away from the unusual concrete box. Then they lifted it up to the floor of the cave.

Allocén traced one finger along the sides of the stone casket with his razor-sharp claw. His claws were sharper than most daggers. The thick talon cut through the sealed stone like it was melted butter. He threw the heavy lid off the box, like when a person flips a quarter with his thumb. It crashed into the wall and shattered into tiny pieces.

For a moment, Allocén sat and stared at the staff that was wrapped in an ancient Jewish blanket. Slowly, he removed the wool material that encased the carved length of wood. The moment he held the relic in his hands, he felt in awe of its power. "We leave for the U. K. in the morning. I've got some very special people to raise from the dead."

Dantanian asked, "Why do we need to raise the dead when we're a hundred times stronger and faster than any mortal?"

"My dear, demonic fool, because we're going to open the gates of hell and start Armageddon. I'll command the Watchers to wreak havoc upon the monkeys our supposed father loves so much. We're going to possess all of humanity one body at a time until there are no uncontaminated souls left. Not even Lucifer can stop me even with the help of his archangel brothers I'll crush them and anyone that stands in my way."

***

Unseen bells rang in Samael's ears. He felt a brief moment of sadness knowing that the sound could signal only one thing; Armageddon was upon humanity.

As he rose from his ebon throne, he could hear the sound of distant trumpets. Gabriel was calling all the Archangels and angel soldiers to the war room in heaven. Just as prophecy foretold, Allocén had discovered the Staff of Moses. He would waste no time before using the staff to open the gates of Hell. The only question was where he would choose to locate the portal.

Michael called for his brother, Samael, "the time has come for our greatest battle. Meet me at the old, abandoned warehouse, on Coney Island Avenue. You know the place where we used to practice sword skills with Dante."

Lucifer noticed that many of the imps and demons that were usually clamoring for his favor had disappeared. They'd also heard the bells and were girding for war. Many had waited eagerly for this day to come and.

His armor stood on a stand in the corner of his favorite torture room. It was heavy, and he wasn't looking forward to wearing it. His sword was mounted above the throne. No demon dared to touch it. They knew if they did so, it meant immediate disintegration.

Armageddon was beginning for humanity and the archangels. He took the sword down and swung it a few times to loosen up. Then, with a single thought, he commanded it to light. Violet and Blue flames ran up the length of the blade. His own dark sight allowed him to see the stronger white flames that danced between the cooler violet and blue that humanity thought was hottest. Most demons only caught a glimpse right before he took their heads.

Most of the stronger archangels were at the warehouse preparing their weapons when he arrived. He could see the surprise in their eyes when he appeared. Most expected him to stand with Hell in the battle.

Barachiel teased his older brother, "Look who decided to come up from sunny Hellville, old Lucifer."

"You're a barrel of laughs, Barachiel. You'll show me respect and address me as Samael." "I apologize brother, I was out of line." "It's okay, We're all not ourselves right now. Prepare yourselves for battle. Michael, where's our son? Has he been told what's transpired?"

"No, Dante is about to engage in battle with Mara. She knows he's the one who spoke with Semyaza while she was driving in the car with the demon. She's not very happy with him."

"What the fuck are we doing here, then? There's no telling how many demons Mara's enlisted to help her kill our son."

"Samael, I've sent Ariel, Asroilu, Chayliel, and Leo to guard him. If the Principalities can't protect him from an invasion of evil angels, then we might as well give up now and say goodbye to Earth. Remember how strong, they are." "I know, they're the Guardian Angels of cities, nations, and rulers. I 've heard it a million times over."

"Well, that should make you feel somewhat better." "But, you know, no angel can protect him better than we can."

"Yes, Samael, I agree. But we've received our orders from Father and must obey them."

"I know, but I don't have to like it. I'll protect my family at all costs, even if I must slaughter everything that stands between us. You've got my solemn promise on that."

Michael knew he would do it. Samael cared about very few things. Dante, Carolyn and his grandchildren were at the top of the list. Michael shouted out his commands to the angels. "Brothers and sisters, we're about to defend heaven and earth from the most demonic fallen ones, and whatever scum they've brought back from the dead. We have no idea where they'll open the portal, but chances are they'll choose one of the larger cities. They want the greatest number of deaths in the shortest amount of time. Hold the line and let nothing get by us. Prepare for battle, it will be upon us in the coming hours."

***

Mara shouted upstairs to the children. "Let's go, we're going to be late for the recital."

Dante's daughter had been chosen to represent her dance school in the district championship. She'd practiced her steps faithfully for weeks and was now ready to perform the intricate dance in the competition. Her mother's words surprised her. She hadn't expected her to attend the exhibition.

Dante was checking his tie in the mirror when he heard his kids trampling down the stairs. "Hey, slow down, someone is going to get hurt." Dante called out. He looked back in the mirror for one last check and noticed his green eyes looked brighter than normal. "Hmm, I wonder what that's all about?" Then he heard the harridan ask his daughter. "What the hell are you supposed to be, a streetwalker? What's with the lipstick and the glitter on your face, you look like a fucking tramp. Go wash that shit off now, young lady"

"Mom, I can't, this is what Mrs. Davis told us to wear."

"Go now, and wash it off, and never talk back to me again." Then he'd heard Mara smack his daughter violently across her face.

Almost simultaneously, there was a knock at the front door.

His daughter was crying. Her makeup was running and the silver glitter ran down her cheek, which was already swelling from the blow.

Dante rushed to her side and saw Mara's palm print on her cheek. He touched her cheek, and the bruise disappeared, then kissed her forehead. He felt them enter before he saw them. "Kids, sit down on the floor where you are. Close your eyes and don't open them until I tell you to."

The two demons were standing in the living room. Both were fallen archangels, and both were fully armed.

"Focalor," he addressed the angel with griffin wings, "what brings you here? Last thing I heard; you were still drilling troops in Hell." "Things change Dante. Your father is no longer in charge." He turned to the other demon who looked like a human with bat wings. "Help Mara with the children."

Dante's eyes darkened. "That would be a serious mistake."

Mara laughed, "what are you going to do about it, convict?" Her eyes widened as Dante's brilliant green eyes changed. His left eye turned the color of fresh blood and the right eye turned indigo blue. His heart surged, sending endorphin enriched blood throughout his arms and chest. He could feel his wings expanding, trying to break free. While keeping one eye on the two fallen ones, he moved lighting fast over to Mara and clamped his hand around the front of her throat. His fingers tightened and squeezed until she cried out to him. Her feet were dangling several inches above the ground. He'd lifted her higher, so he could look directly into her panic-stricken eyes.

"If you ever touch my children again, witch, I'll take your last fucking breath from you."

As if his anger was a signal, Mara opened her hand. Then she swung it across his face, cutting deep gashes on his cheek with her razor tip claws.

Dante cursed as the blood flowed down his face. He shook Mara again, then threw her across the room, knocking her unconscious. He turned around quickly when he heard the two demons moving towards the children.

"No!" he screamed. There was a sudden surge of pain in back as his wings tore through the final layer of skin. He extended his hand toward the wooden chest his fathers had given him. The everlasting chains flew out from the chest and wrapped around his forearm. Like in the movie Raiders of the Lost Ark, he snapped the chain in a whipping motion toward the two demons, smiling as the magical links coiled around Focalor's neck. In a husky voice he announced, "There'll be no darkness for you." He gave the everlasting chains a violent tug and snapped it, decapitating the senior demon. His head rolled across the floor, stopping near Mara's body. Focalor's soul loomed in the air, the thick black cloud searched for a vessel to enter and took aim for Dante's oldest son. Dante sent the everlasting chains in its direction and destroyed Focalor's soul. He then inhaled his grace.

Gaap tried to run, but Dante was ready for him. The chains whipped out, striking him between the wings as he tried to escape. He tumbled to the floor at Dante's feet. He kicked the demon in the temple, knocking him unconscious. The chains instantly wrapped back around his arm again.

Mara crouched beside the wall, trembling in fear. She looked at her former lover, recognizing that he was a Nephilim. She knew he was the chosen one written about in Lilith's book of Immortals. Now terrified, she pleaded with him to let her go.

Dante had no intention of releasing either of them. "Mara, you've been charged with treason against the almighty father and sentenced to life in the darkness." With that, he inhaled what little grace remained in the human vessel she'd picked to live in. He pulled the injured demon to his feet and shoved him to the ground by Mara, he whipped the chains around both bodies, and banished them into the darkness.

Once everything in the room looked normal, he turned and spoke to his children. His voice was much deeper and raspy. "Fear not, little ones, you're safe now." He touched their foreheads saying, "forget what thy have seen here today and worry not. I'm your father and protector from all evil." Then he tapped each of their foreheads and they fell asleep instantly.

***

Michael felt the disturbance in the ether as Dante manifested his destiny. He yelled over to Samael, who was already heading in his direction. "It's happened. We need to go… now" Gabriel and Raphael followed them. The room illuminated and the four archangels stood in awe of their son and nephew, the newest archangel.

"My lord, he's magnificent," Samael shouted with joy.

"Yes, brother, he's the perfect combination of angel and human, isn't he? Look at what we've created and given life." Gabriel went over to Dante and said, "You need to retract your wings. The power is like a gigantic red arrow pointing directly at this house. Relax, focus on calming your heart rate and blood pressure." Dante closed his eyes and tried to blank out his mind. Gradually, he morphed back into his normal self. His eyes returned to their normal color green. The endomorphic surge had left his body.

"What took place here, son?" Samael inquired. "Mara struck my daughter. I healed the bruise on my little girl's cheek and then the change happened. My eyes turned red and blue. It amplified my vision a hundred times stronger than normal. It was as if I could see miles ahead of me and I was so focused. I grabbed Mara by the throat, and told her, 'I'd take the very last breath from her body' if she ever harmed my kids again. That's when the two demons started to move toward the kids. The children say it's not the first time they came into the house. Mara called them her helpers.

When Focalor and Gaap charged at me, my wings broke through my back and extended outward. I vaguely remember pointing to the wooden chest and calling for the chains. They shot out and wrapped around my arm. I passed judgement on both demons. I ruled death and decapitated Focalor. Gaap and Mara, I banished into the Darkness. I inhaled Mara's and Focalor's grace and destroyed Focalor's soul. It was trying to enter my oldest son's body.

Michael spoke next. "You handed down the judgment of death? That's unheard of. Only Phanuel, the minister of judgement, may do that."

"Well, I don't know how I did it, but it's done. Am I in any kind of trouble with grandfather or Phanuel?"

Gabriel shrugged. "No, Dante, if you were, you'd already have been punished. You're a true justice keeper and we now know for sure that one of your other duties is to be heaven and hell's enforcer."

"How's he going to do all of this?" Samael asked. "He's mostly going to be on earth being heaven and hell's exorcist."

"When he's needed to be the justice keeper, he'll know it. He's a big angel now," Michael said, laughing.

They all had a brief laugh. Michael went

and retrieved Carolyn and explained what had happened. "You'll have to help Dante with raising the children."

"Of course, I'll help him raise them, they're our grandchildren."

"Samael and I will assist you whenever we can, my love"

"I know, my sweet angel."

He looked down at his granddaughter. "Is there something I missed?"

"Yes," she announced. "If we don't leave now, we're going to be late for my recital!"

***

Newgate Prison Cemetery held the remains of hundreds of England's deadliest criminals. Allocén and his two cohorts stood before the grave of Doctor Neill Thomas Crem, a man known as the true Jack the Ripper. He'd been busy reviving a select few humans around the UK to help him achieve his goals, and the doctor was on his list. He held out the staff and shouted, "Arise Neill Crem and be born again, do my bidding as Jack the Ripper." The ground rumbled beneath their feet and the headstone exploded into pieces. Out from the grave came a hand.

Asmodeus extended his hand and helped pull Crem out of the grave. The reborn killer reached back into the ground and retrieved his top hat. After dusting away the dirt that was clinging to the hat and his suit, he let out a cough and a cloud of dust came out of his mouth. "My, my, that was a very unpleasant time down there. To whom do I owe this debt"

Allocén's smile was more of a smirk than anything pleasant. "That would be I, doctor, or should I call you Mr. Ripper."

"Damn, the cats out of the bag, ay gents." His eyes scanned his rescuer up and down, noting the claws on his large hand. Things had changed a bit since they hung him. He wondered how long he'd been in Newgate Cemetery but wasn't sure he should ask. These demonic looking creatures didn't look particularly friendly or informative.

"Doctor, we're not of this world, we're the Watchers, the Fallen Ones. You'll serve me and wreak unholy hell upon the monkeys that roam White Chapel. Do you understand? Or will one of my friends behind me have to kill you again?" Crem looked into Allocén's eyes and saw death. "You, sir, have a deal. May I get a change of clothes and perhaps a hot shower? Maybe a little food and drink?"

"Be my guest, now go slaughter the whores like old times."

The three demons watched as the doctor scrambled across the overgrown field, heading back into London.

"Think you made a mistake with that one? He didn't seem as willing to kill as some of the others." Said Dantanian.

"Trust me. He is one of the best. I intend to keep an eye on him, if only to enjoy how he dispenses pain while mutilating the women's bodies."

There was a brief moment of silence, and then Dantanian asked, "where to next, Allocén?"

"Mary Hill Cemetery in Illinois. We've got a date, with a clown, my friend."

"Don't tell me… we are going after another serial killer."

"Of course, why raise a beginner when we can call back an expert."

"But a Killer Clown?"

"This is an unusual case. He claimed his name was Jack, and he killed young men and boys after having sex with them. No one could ever figure out why he talked about the killer as if it was someone besides himself. I'm curious if it was the spirit of Jack the Ripper occupying his body. Since we just animated Jack the Ripper, he can't possibly be in two places at one time. So, we'll either lose the good doctor or get a killer clown and the ripper."

Unlike London, this cemetery was clean and well maintained. They had no trouble locating the correct grave. The headstone was smaller than some of the others, but they carved his name into the granite.

"This one hasn't been in the ground as long as the good doctor." Allocén said as they walked up to the grave.

Dantanian quickly scattered the salt around the outside perimeter while Allocén waited impatiently for him to finish. Once the gate was complete, he touched the ground with the staff and called forth his clown.

"O' Hear' ye I command John Wayne Gacy, arise from the dirt and ashes and be my killing servant, arise. "

Gacy crawled out from beneath the earth and shook his clown suit off. "Damn it, where's my clown nose? Ah, I know where I hid it. Excuse me while I retrieve it." They watched as the clown went back into the hole. Seconds later, Gacy reappeared with his red nose attached to his face. He was holding a butcher's knife. "Show me where the boys are so I can get to the chopping."

"You don't give orders here, clown boy. Now take a seat on that fucking bench and listen to my commands," Allocén said. "I've got a question. Why did you tell the judge and police your name was Jack?"

"I figured they might go easier on me if they thought I was insane. Only a really crazy person would claim to be Jack the Ripper."

The three demons began to laugh. They stopped maintaining their human aspects and revealed their full demonic appearance.

John Wayne trembled when the three demons showed their true selves. "You'll do my bidding. Is that understood, Johnny boy?"

"Yeah, I mean yes. Yes sir. What the hell do I call you, anyway?"

"You can call me, Duke; I'm the Duke of Hell. Now leave and go murder as many young men as you can."

By day's end Allocén had resurrected Peter Sutcliffe the Yorkshire ripper, Harold Shipman, Dennis Nilsen the Muswell Hill Murderer, Ted Bundy, two men who claimed to be the Zodiac Killer, Ed Gein, Albert Fish the American Cannibal, and the BTK Killer, Dennis Rader. He gave each of them strict orders. "Go out and kill and kill some more." They were his murderers' row of serial killers.

"Now we head back to Hell and recruit all the fallen, to do battle against heaven's Archangels. Asmodeus can gather all his witches and warlocks. Dantanian, you can round up all the lesser demons and cacodemons. We'll need them all."

He looked around at the millions of humans and smiled. "Everyone will eat well once I've opened the gates of hell."

PART - FOUR

Dante sat with his kids and mother in her kitchen. She'd baked a nice lasagna and he'd eaten two helpings, knowing damn well, it might very well be his last supper with them. He opened the chest and inside were the everlasting chains, an archangel sword, a dagger with angelic sigils and runes on the blade. Under a blanket were two 357 magnum revolvers in shoulder holsters.

Michael appeared moments later and placed his hand on his son's shoulder. "Dante, open your hands, these are 357 magnum armor – piercing bullets that were cast from the metal of our archangels' swords. You must use them with caution. You can't run to the gun and ammo shop for more. When you fire at a demon you need to hit it center mass or higher. This will permanently execute them."

Dante carefully loaded the guns with the special bullets, placing the rest in the chest. "Thank you, father," "I've got a question.

After you killed the two fallen ones, how did you destroy their souls and consume their grace?"

Michael looked puzzled. "How's that even possible? No arch has those powers."

"I'm not sure. When they died their souls traveled through the air and I used the chains and cut through them, then their grace entered me. I felt a surge of power for a few seconds, and I knew it was over and they no longer existed."

"Dante, you've got to be careful with these powers. They'll tempt you to fall, and the demonic grace will take over inside you."

"I'll use them wisely; I swear on our holy father."

"Go and kiss your mother and children goodbye, we must prepare for the great war. Ariel and Cerviel have volunteered to protect

Carolyn and the children."

"I know Ariel, but who is Cerviel?"

"He's the angel ruler of the Principalities. They're in good hands; they're two of God's greatest soldiers."

Dante kissed his mother goodbye and went over to talk to his children. He kneeled on one knee, so he'd be at eye level with them. "You know, I love you more than anything in the world, right?"

"Yes, daddy, where are you going? Can we come with you?"

"Not today kids, I'll be back as soon as I can. Behave for grandma. Your uncles will watch over you until I return." He kissed them on their foreheads, and said, "goodbye my precious ones, I love you all." Then he vanished.

***

Allocen sat on Lucifer's throne, preparing to make a speech to his demon soldiers. They were approaching the apex of the ongoing battle, and he needed them to be ready for any attempt to thwart his plans. "My fellow, fallen ones, the time has come to reclaim our rightful place in heaven and to rule hell. First, we'll destroy the Archangels. Then we will subjugate all of humanity. I command you to possess as many humans as possible. We'll rule heaven and hell, keeping only enough humans to serve as our slaves. Imagine being able to fuck all the beautiful women on earth. Our sex slaves will give birth to our offspring. I'll be the ruler of all nations. Are you with me?"

Most of the demons raised their weapons and swore their allegiance to Allocen. There was a band of devoted demons who stood by the Grand Duke of Hell, Astaroth. He had other plans to destroy humanity and wasn't happy to see so many supporting Alloccen's campaign.

Allocen approached the Grand Duke and bowed his head respectfully. "Master, do I have your blessing to proceed with my plans?"

Astaroth thought about his answer. Destroying the archangels wouldn't be as easy as Allocen made it sound. Many demons would not survive the upcoming battle. With luck, Allocen would be one of the lost. If not, he'd worry about what to do with the power-hungry Duke once he returned. "Go now and wreak hell on the archangels. When they're no longer a threat, we'll break the seal and throw open the gates of hell together."

With that, Allocen led his legion of demons and they ascended to earth.

The killers that were resurrected began their killing spree of the innocents. The Ripper dismembered women in London while Bundy, Gacy and the others murdered men and women in the United States. The Duke of Hell had resurrected forty of the most sanguine killers.

Dantanian was enjoying the mayhem.

"Should we resurrect anymore?"

"I think that'll do for now. Law enforcement authorities will have their hands full trying to apprehend my Newborn's. I'm their new father and king. I need you to bring me the evilest bloodthirsty of demons. We'll no longer be called the Fallen Ones. We're the Watchers and will forever be known as the demons from hell. Now, go and gather the evilest of demons. Tell Abaddon and Morax they've been appointed to be the two squadron Captains. We leave tonight."

He paused and then added, "if anyone spots Lucifer, he's to be taken alive and brought back to me in chains,"

"That's a suicide mission he'll destroy us within seconds. I agreed to follow you and help locate Moses' staff. I also agreed to fight as long as we have reinforcements with us."

"Then take more reinforcement with you and capture him."

"I won't do it, he's the king of hell and our true master." Dantanian shouted.

Allocen moved with lighting speed and pinned him against the wall. "You'll do as I command, or I'll rip you into pieces. Then I'll slaughter your lady love on earth. The tramp you think no one knew about."

Dantanian remained silent for a minute.

Allocen's eyes turned deep red. Then he shouted, "bring her to me, Asmodeus."

Asmodeus walked into the room, dragging the naked woman by her hair.

Dantanian heard his lover screaming.

Asmodeus gloated as he moved his grip to her throat and squeezed. In seconds, her fragile neck was going to break.

Dantanian knew he had no options except to obey. "Alright, my lord, you've made your point. I'm yours to command. Let her go, please."

"I'm glad you've reconsidered. I'll keep her down here with us, until we're victorious. Now, go and locate the turncoat Lucifer and bring him to me."

***

Michael was going over the strategics of his plans with the Archs and the other angels.

Dante, called to his father Samael. "Father,

I'm ready to fight against the Fallen Ones."

Samael appeared behind him and tapped his shoulder. "So, what's the holdup then? Get your ass over to the abandoned building on Coney Island Avenue. That's where the other angels are preparing for battle".

"Father I'll drive us there."

"You silly little angel, take them for a trial run. Push your wings out, and leap into the air." He laughed. "Don't forget to keep flapping your wings, it hurts when you hit the ground."

Dante stepped outside to give himself more room. He pulled his stomach in and breathed deeply. Seconds later his white wings spread wide, and he pushed them in a downward motion and was lifted off the ground.

Samael clapped and yelled, "I'm proud of you, son, I'll meet you there before nightfall. Let Michael know, I've got one last mission in hell to complete for my father."

Dante turned around and jetted towards the ground, but his father had already descended into hell. "Shit, I hate it when he does that."

He knew if he'd followed Samael, there would be a good chance he wouldn't make it out alive. He was still learning about his new powers and the fighting skills he'd recently acquired. His father was right, flying was more fun than driving and much faster. He shrugged and went to look for Michael.

***

Dantanian stepped as tactically as he could into the part of hell known as Lucifer's 'Den of Torture'. He expected Lucifer would return here to complete the conditioning of the latest batch of damned souls. Whenever there was an especially deranged homicidal soul that needed special attention, Lucifer carried out the initial torture. This was something he was not fond of, but he had his orders from heaven. He knew Lucifer was proud of one thing, unlike most of hell's residents, he never lied to anyone in his life. That's not to say that he wouldn't tempt you with every desire he could devise. Those were God's orders; he was the balance of mankind.

Lucifer was taking a break when Dantanian came up behind him, but he knew he was there. "Hello Dantanian, what brings you to my little pleasure palace in hell? I expected you to be wreaking havoc up top with Allocen and Asmodeus."

"My lord, you disparage me. Why would I risk your anger?"

"Really? What reason would such an evil yet beautiful angel like yourself, have to be afraid of little old me? I've been hearing very disturbing rumors. It seems some rebellious demons are looking to dethrone me and claim hell for themselves."

Lucifer turned so he could look eye to eye with Dantanian. "Your name was mentioned several times. What do you know of this plan, Dantanian? And don't, fucking lie me? I hate liars."

"My king, I know nothing of what you speak."

"That's strike one, you, disobedient bastard"

Before Dantanian could register his movement, Samael opened his hand and sent a furious smack across the disloyal demon's face.

"There's nothing worse than being smacked in the face rather than punched. Isn't that true you fucking perfidious little prick. Now that you've made me so angry, you've got two strikes against you. Lie to me again and I'll not only bring my wrath down upon you, but heavens as well." He took a second to gather his emotions before asking, "What are the rebels planning against the Archangels and the Nephilim?"

Dantanian shifted his weight uncomfortably. He'd never seen Lucifer this angry. "Many hate all the archangels, but nothing makes a demon angrier than the Nephilim."

"The Nephilim who happens to be my only son?"

"Did you say the half breed is your son, Lucifer?" Dantanian's dark red skin paled to a washed out pink.

Lucifer's eye's flashed yellow as he transformed into the beast known as the devil. He heard the voice of God telling him, "Don't my son, don't do what you're about to do. Otherwise, everything we've worked for will be for nothing. Dantanian hasn't challenged you or fought back. Use the everlasting chains and send him into the darkness. Remember you're my beloved son, and my first Justice Keeper."

Lucifer raised his hand into the air and roared. "Chains of Justice, I've rendered the judgement of darkness for this disloyal fallen one." The chains appeared as a huge serpent and wrapped around his arm. "I Samael, the first archangel who became Lucifer the king of hell sentenced you, Dantanian, into the darkness for life."

Before the demon could beg or plead his case, Samael cast the chains onto him.

As the demon was being dragged away by the serpent into the darkness, he yelled, "Allocen and Asmodeus are behind this treachery. Please spare my lady love, they hold her under guard to guarantee my obedience. Please protect her from them."

The demon was gone. Lucifer's justice chains returned and wrapped around his chest like a bandolier. He called up to his brother. "Michael, I'm coming up, I've confirmed who's behind this coup attempt."

"Hurry Samael, things are getting bad up here, the end of time is upon us."

Gabriel and Uriel had called in their elite team of angels, a special platoon known as the Powers. Their vocation was to prevent the fallen from taking over the world and keeping the universe balanced. They gave the gathered Powers their orders, "Seek out the abominations that were returned to life and by any means necessary send those sadistic killers back to hell."

Dante assembled his war gear; his arch sword and dagger were razor sharp. He checked his revolvers and spun the cylinders to ensure every chamber was loaded and then shut them with a flick of his wrist. He wore the two shoulder holsters crisscrossed which would enable him to grab the guns quickly. The specially designed guns would only operate with his palm prints. The everlasting chains were sitting on his right hip ready to administer judgement on the invading army of demons. Michael called the Archangels to the war room. Samael and Dante stood to his left and right. "It's been a millennium since we've had to use all our full powers and strength to fight. Tonight, we'll need every ounce of them. Samael has confirmed it's the Duke Allocen and Asmodeus that are commanding the hordes from hell."

Night had fallen, and they'd stepped outside. A brilliant bright light lit the sky. When it finally dimmed the other angel soldiers had witnessed the true form of the Archangels. They observed seven stunning looking giant figures that were wearing Spartan helmets and gold-plated vests which were inscribed with glyphs and sigils. The Archangels were at least eighty feet tall, and their wingspan was as wide as a jetliner. Their voices were now very deep and raspy.

Michael spoke calmly but his voice was loud as a shout. "Archers, take your battle positions. Scouts, begin your recon and signal every ten minutes back to your squadron captains."

Samael roared with his Archdemon voice, "Foot soldiers form a triangular wedge. We've been issued high kill orders from our father. None of the fallen are to be spared. It is the almighty father's will that they all be destroyed or sent into the darkness.

Raphael moved to command his troops, "Principalities, take your griffins and fly overhead. Protect the foot soldiers."

Dante's hand squeezed the hilt of his sword. His eyes hadn't transformed yet. He'd quickly mastered the transformation process of becoming an archangel and was able to control it with ease. The training Michael and Samael had instilled in him, when he was young, had truly paid off.

It was around midnight when the ground shook like an earthquake and in seconds an army of demons came out of the ground which had split open. They started their attack on the angels. The principalities soared down toward the enemy, and quickly took out ten heavenly armed demons. The demons fought back and took a heavy toll. Asmodeus swung a heavy hammer like the one Thor used in the comics, bashing the heads of three of the Griffins, killing them instantly. He then stood over the Principalities that were injured and crushed their skulls into pulp.

Dante had heard one of the Griffins squealing in horrendous pain. As he looked up, he saw Asmodeus lifting his great hammer. He hurled his dagger into the demon's left eye. Dante did the switch and his arms and chest swelled as his heart furiously pumped blood. He kept his wings suppressed until he knew he'd need them most. He needed to be able to move freely during battle.

Asmodeus pulled the knife out from his skull with the eyeball still attached to the dagger. He removed it and popped into his mouth and swallowed it. Then he hurled the dagger back at Dante, who easily caught it and placed it back into its holder. He bolted towards Dante screaming, "I'll kill you, half breed." As he approached Dante he swung the hammer at the Nephilim's head, but Dante ducked and thrust his sword under the demon's chin and ran his blade through Asmodeus' skull.

Dante inhaled the demon's grace and obliterated his soul with the chains of justice, ensuring there was no way he could be resurrected by the staff. The battle raged on for hours. Raphael had been badly injured and wasn't healing and needed to be taken back up to heaven for medical treatment.

Allocen had raised more killers to assist him in the battle. That was creating a problem for the Archangels. They were forbidden to kill a human, but Samael implored his brothers. "They've already been dead once before. Killing them now isn't against father's rules. Their souls have already been judged. Now kill them, or we'll suffer many casualties. Fight for heaven and humanity like we were commanded to do."

Dante and Michael took the attack to the resurrected killers and slaughtered ten of them within thirty seconds. The tide was turning in their favor. It wouldn't be long before they fought their way to Allocen. Once they removed the instigator, the remaining demons could easily be dispatched or retreat back into hell.

Suddenly Samael's ears rang in pain, sending sharp pain throughout his body. He knew it could only mean one thing; Carolyn and his grandchildren were in great danger. He struggled to overcome the pain and alerted Dante and Michael of the danger.

Gabriel yelled to them, "Go and protect the family. We've got this under control."

Dante immediately called forth his wings, Then the three angels spread their wings and took flight. Michael was flying above Samael and Dante and observed his son's wings had blood on them. Then he realized it was coming from Samael who was flying above Dante. "Samael, you're bleeding, where are you hit, and how bad is it?"

"One of the demons must've gotten ahold of Raphael's arch blade. He ran it into the lower part of my abdomen when the bells rang, they distracted me. It went in and out through my back."

"Let's land, I'll heal you."

"There's no time for that, Carolyn and the children are in great danger. Their lives mean more than mine."

Michael didn't argue with his older brother, but he was worried about him. The cut might not kill him, but the pain would be a constant distraction at a time when they needed to be at their best. Allocen crashed through Carolyn's roof and swung the stolen archangel blade across Ariel throat before he had a chance to raise his weapon. Cerviel tried to defend the family, but Allocen was a better swordman. In the matter of minutes Cerviel was on the ground bleeding heavily and dying. Allocen made his way over to Carolyn and the children.

"So, you're the bitch who gave birth to the Nephilim. Who may I ask are these little bastards?" Carolyn stood in front of her grandchildren. "Leave them be, they're innocent and have nothing to do with this, leave them out of it."

"You, don't give me orders, you little monkey." He sent a backhand across her face, which sent her into the wall knocking her out. Allocen showed his true form, and the children were terrified of the demon's face. It was a grotesque mixture of a lion and bull. He leaned closer and sniffed the three children. "Hmm, looks like you little monkeys are hybrids, like your daddy. Strange combination a Nephilim and a witch. I'm tempted to see if one of you can be turned. This is going to be a glorious slaughter of the divine family. He took a step forward, then stopped as Dante came gliding through the opening Allocen had torn in the roof of his mother's home. "So, you're the big kahuna half breed, huh. Tell you what, just surrender to me and let me drain your blood and consume your soul. Then I'll spare your little angels." Michael and Samael landed on the left- and right-hand side of their son. "That's not going to happen, Allocen, I'm sending you into the darkness where you belong,"

Samael raised his sword and gestured the Archduke to come closer.

"Lucifer the O" almighty king of hell, has turned his back on his loyal servants and betrayed us all. How does it feel to be a scum sucking human loving traitor?"

"You, filthy scumbag, my brother never wanted any of that shit down in hell.

He was chosen to be the judge and prosecutor of sinners by our father."

"Enough talk, monkey lovers, time for you and your Nephilim scum to die." Allocen raised the staff and shouted, in his demonic voice, "Watchers and demonic beings come and assist me in delivering the final death blow to the Archangels." Three Watches came crashing into the house. Botis, looked more like a viper than a demon. However, Ipos was clearly an angel with a lion's head and both archangels knew the shifter Flauros from before he fell.

Upon seeing who he would be fighting, Flauros immediately shifted into a giant leopard and maneuvered behind the other two demons.

"Attack, my faithful ones and tear their grace out from within them," Allocen shouted.

Botis and Ipos took the fight to the Archangels closest to them.

Samael and Michael transformed again and towered over the demons. Blazing swords in hand. Dante let the beast out from within him and the Justice Keepers began to battle. Michael slammed his mighty sword down upon Botis's head and sliced in a downward motion, cutting him completely in half. As he was dying, Botis' grace tried to enter Dante's daughter, but the Justice keeper was too quick and absorbed the demon's grace obliterating the black soul that was looming over his daughter's head.

Flauros had noticed the blood on Samael's back and decided he stood a better chance fighting with Ipos against the injured archangel.

Samael grinned, knowing they had no idea what they were in for. The reason Dante entered first, was so Michael could take the time to heal his brother's injury.

Samael grabbed Flauros's thick leopard fur and picked him up off the ground. Then he snapped his fingers, making the fallen one, explode. Without a body, the demon was banished from Earth, but it would be waiting when he returned to his duties in hell. Keeping an eye on Allocen at all times, he drove his fist into Ipos stomach, causing the demon to lose his blade. Samael kicked it away from him and then threw Ipos across the room. The winged cat hit the floor and slid several feet before coming to a stop at Dante's feet.

Dante immediately then pulled the Everlasting chains off his hip and passed judgement on the demon, "I sentence you to life in the darkness, evil one." Ipos disappeared and seconds later the chains returned to Dante's hip.

Allocen started to clap his hands saying, "Did you fools think that's all I had up my sleeve?" He let out a loud roar and commanded the resurrected ones to assist him in killing Dante's children and mother. The worst killers known to mankind came rushing through the doors of Carolyn's home. Allocen knew the rules and code of the Archangels. "Too bad you can't interfere or kill a human."

Michael smiled as he lopped off one of the killer's head. "That's true. But that doesn't stop us from returning humans who'd already been dead to their graves. They've already been judged, and their souls forfeited. They're simply walking skin sacks now. The three Justice keepers annihilated all the serial killers in the matter of seconds.

During the battle they'd lost eye contact with the kids and Carolyn. As Dante's blade struck the final blow, they heard the scream of the youngest child. Allocen held the boy in the air and opened his mouth wide to consume him. Dante rushed over to help his son, but Allocen extended the staff and threw him across the room. His body smashed a hole in the sheetrock and broke several two by fours before coming to a stop against a bed in the next room.

Samael darted between his beloved Carolyn and grandchildren and began his assault on the demon. He'd taken his demonic form again and became a blood thirsty monster. He spoke in angelic/demon tongue, "you, dare to challenge me, the king of hell? Suffer my wrath and be no more." His sword knocked the blade from Allocen's hand.

Forced to make a decision between killing the boy and dying or releasing him and fighting Samael, Allocen tossed the child away.

Michael made a diving catch right before the child would have crashed through the plate glass window.

Samael was furious Allocen would endanger his grandchild in that manner. He extended his talons and sent his clawed hand into the ribcage of the Demon Duke, ripping his still beating heart from his chest. The duke's grace and soul entered the air and was traveling towards the kids. "Dante, take his grace now before it possesses one of the children."

Dante stood between the dead demon and the children and sucked the grace from the air into his lungs and whipped the everlasting chains out and destroyed his evil soul. Everyone was talking at one time. Dante had the children in his arms and Michal was trying to clean the gore from Carolyn's bloodstained face. Samael returned to his human form and was resting against the arm of the sofa holding Carolyn's hand.

There was an incredible bright flash of light and a burst of demonic power as the Grand Duke of Hell, Astaroth appeared. Things happened quickly, Samael stepped in front of Carolyn and his grandchildren to protect them. He wrapped his wings around them just as Astaroth hurled a trident directly at Carolyn.

The trident was made from an original stolen Archangel blade. It went through Samael's wings coming to rest partway through his chest. Astaroth snatched up the staff of Moses and fled with the staff in hand back into hell. Around the universe the Archangels felt a current go through them. It could only mean that one of their brothers were dying. Carolyn and the children were hugging Samael and crying. Michael tried to heal the massive wound.

The other Archangels appeared and knelt beside Samael and stayed with him, until it was time to go home. He tried to smile as he looked into their faces. "This isn't a time for tears, you're my family and I told you all, I'd always protect you, even if it meant my death. I'm your oldest brother and that's my duty. I love you all." He reached out to his grandchildren. "My beautiful babies, you're the light of my life. My beautiful son and beloved Carolyn you two are my heart and soul forever." His black wings faded and turned pearl white, and he was taken up to heaven. His true home.

Michael cried uncontrollably. He was consoled by the other angels and his grandchildren, but the pain of his loss would not ease.

Gabriel whispered into his ear. "We must leave now Michael; Dante will take care of things down here. We need to be with father and prepare for our brother's funeral." One of the other Archangel's named Selaphiel touched the children's foreheads and they fell asleep. "Remember none of what you've seen tonight." They all disappeared, and Dante helped his mother up off the floor and consoled her grief until she fell asleep.

Several days had passed and Dante felt the earth rumble. He knew it was beginning again. He was sitting in the back yard watching the flames dancing around in the fire pit. He felt an archangel's presence and then a bright light shone in his eyes. Moments later Michael and Gabriel appeared. "We've got a surprise for you; go get your mother and the kids."

They all sat around the fire and a cluster of stars exploded in the sky. It was magnificent to look at. They heard a joyous voice from the sky; it was their great grandfather, the father, almighty. Beautiful harp music was playing above as he spoke. "My beautiful family, this is my son, my first creation and my beloved Samael, he's the protector of all my angels."

Samael was dressed in golden warrior armor etched and engraved with sigils and glyphs of power. He glided over them with his white stunning wings. Then he floated slowly down to the ground.

Michael said, "Oh, my goodness, did you have to be so dramatic about it?"

"Of course, I did, it wouldn't be me, if I didn't exaggerate things. Besides they thought I was gone forever. "He opened his arms, "Who here, missed, their favorite grandfather?"

The children rushed into his arms. Carolyn had tears in her eyes, but she stayed calm and waited. Samael wasn't the same. He'd transitioned and she wasn't sure how she should behave around him. She'd only known him as the justice of hell. This bright angel scared her a bit.

Samael smiled and turned to Michael saying, "I love you bro."

Dante was in shock. He'd already accepted the idea of his father's death along with the idea he'd never see him again. Now he wasn't sure what to think. He stared at his father in awe. The grandkids jump all over Samael with joy. They had their pop, pop back. The hours passed, and they ate, drank and joked with each other. Michael took each of the children's pinky's and prick them very lightly and drew a little blood from each of their fingers. Samael, Michael, Raphael, and Gabriel each did the same. Then they put their fingers together and made the blood oath of the archangels. Something that Michael had just made up. Not knowing that all of their powers would combine in the kids later on in their lives.

Dante made the children swear they'd never speak of their angelic grandfathers, and uncles to anyone. Each child stood and held up their little hands and swore they'd never speak of their family with any person.

Once the children were in bed Dante decide he needed answers. "Can we talk? Just the three of us. I'm sure Uncle Gabriel will stay with the family." Raphael had gone back up to be with his father.

Gabriel agreed. He was enjoying a movie and had no intention of leaving until it finished. This was the third time he'd tried to watch the Lord of The Rings trilogy. Since his nephew had all three films, he intended to indulge himself. He laughed to himself saying, "I'm movie binging like the humans do on weekends." He laughed uncontrollably.

Five minutes fathers and son were perched on a ledge overlooking the city. While they had no trouble seeing each other, no one else could see them. The building was one of their favorite meeting spots, with wide comfortable ledges that backed up to a low knee wall that was perfect to lean against.

Dante wasted no time with explanations. Instead, he asked about the rumbling movement the day before. "Did either of you feel the quake beneath our feel yesterday?"

"Yes, we all did. Hell is coming and you Dante, must be prepared." Michael said in a stern voice. "Does that mean Astaroth has used the staff to open the portal between hell and earth or that he's still trying to open it?"

Michael looked at Samael, "We don't know."

***

Astaroth, was standing inside a demonic pentagram he'd cut into rock where he wanted to start his portal. He spoke the commands in an ancient tongue. "Let all the demons and fallen ones, corrupt the earth and all of humanity. We shall possess every man, woman, and child, until humanity is no more. Let the gates of hell be open and free my army of Watchers. Go now, my children and destroy all of them." The pentacle began to glow, and the ground opened. Within seconds the air was thick with demonic bodies as the fallen ones escaped hell. Those with wings soared into the sky and the land was covered with writhing creature of the dark.

"What the fuck was that?" Dante asked. They all looked up and the sky was filled with what appeared to be shooting stars. Michael's eyes grew shallow, and the lines of tension formed on his face.

Samael was already standing as he rose to his feet before answering Dante's question. "I guess the answer is there's no more time. Those lights are the Watches. They've escaped from hell. Astaroth has opened the gates of hell and the armies of cacodemons and demons are coming forth." Samael relayed his father's instruction to his son.

"Dante, you need to go to Rome now. It's important that you meet with Pope John the fourth tonight. He'll initiate you as an exorcist priest with the Roman Catholic church. Hurry, time is of the essence."

The archangels knew a lot of innocent humans would die before Dante returned from Rome. They decided the first thing to do was get their family to a safe location, there was a church in the city with a priest that was spiritually closer to God than any other in the United States. That wouldn't stop the demon horde, but they would certainly postpone their attempts to overrun the church until all the easier targets were destroyed. Their family would be safer there than any other place. Michael suggested it to Samael and his brother agreed. While Dante was busy in Rome, they'd be busy fighting demons down on earth. All they could do is hope to keep as many humans as possible alive until their son returned.

Rome was nothing like Dante expected. They were extremely technical and had one of the largest libraries he'd ever seen. For several months he was trained in the rites of exorcism by the best priests Rome had to offer. The Pope explained to him. "There are several levels of exorcisms my son. It's said that the first exorcism was by one of the Archangel's, he cast out a devil from a town carpenter. He expelled the demon into a dessert in Egypt"

Dante decided it might not be good to mention Samael was one of his father's. The pope was having enough difficulty dealing with a real Nephilim and the assorted demons reported in the streets of Rome.

The pope continued by saying, "another stage is oppression. The influence of a demonic force or being which comes from outside a person causing heaviness, weariness or discouragement. The oppressive sprits might be acquired through exposure to a heavy presence of evil, by participating in an occult or unholy mass. The person can become cursed by witchcraft because they've encountered a demonic sprit or a black witch. These oppressed sprits can be expelled by a simple command to leave in the name of our lords' son."

That was easy enough to remember, cast them out in J's name. Got it.

"Next there's obsession, the demonic influence which resides in a person. A man or woman can open themselves up to an underworld demon and strike a bargain at a crossroad. That deal will have a heavy price attached to it, for that person. It usually requires the subject to give up their soul to the demon they've struck the deal with. The contract holder owns them when they die and they always go to hell."

He paused and looked at his student. Dante nodded. "I understand, your greatness."

"Finally, there's possession. It's rare and can come about in two ways. One, the person willfully agrees to hand over their will to Satan. By doing so they've committed a grave sin against our heavenly father. Witches and Warlocks often bind their soul in this manner. The other way is a higher-ranking demon has entered the body of a pure soul and tries to destroy it from within. You must get the demon to say its name, before the person is killed by the possession. Once you know the demons name you can exorcise it out and save the possessed person. You'll be strictly dealing with possessions, Dante. The evilest demons that roam the earth. Study hard and be resilient and forge ahead. Michael and Gabriel told me to remind you you're, Heaven and Hells exorcist, and its final Justice Keeper. By the way Dante, I know who your other father is and how he sacrificed his life for Carolyn and your children. I know Samael is the light bearer and what he was charged to do for so many centuries. When you see him, please give him my regards and tell him, thank you for all he's done for us down here."

Dante signed. He spent the last month with Father Charlie exorcising demons who'd possessed the men, women and children in Rome. He realized he knew most of what the priests had offered, and his training was complete. He kept reciting the words of the exorcist bible every chance he had. The Pope had told him. "This is just the beginning Dante. Hell has opened its doors on us. Be ready, the time is now upon you to save humanity."

Dante was finally ready to return home to his children. He needed a few hours rest while things were still reasonably quiet. The priests had invited him to share one of the penitents' chambers, a small closet size room with a twin bed and little else inside. He had no idea how long he'd been sleeping when he heard a young woman cry out from another place unknown to him. He sat up and got dressed. He didn't know why he needed to go to the girl. He only knew he had to go immediately. He said his goodbyes and flew away.

***

Gina Cappelletti was 16 going on 21. She was an A student in school and had never been in trouble. She was respectful to her parents and teachers. Just an all-around sweet teenager. She'd not been feeling well the past few days and was running a high fever. Her mother Gale had finally gotten her to fall asleep. Gale and her husband Chris were watching TV downstairs when they'd heard what they thought was the family dog coming down the stairs. But it wasn't the dog. It was Gina.

Her body was bent and contorted. Her limbs had twisted completely around, so that her hands had now become front legs. Her head was spun around and she was looking at them upside down. She walked on her hands and feet like a four-legged animal. Her pale blue eyes were now scarlet red and she spoke in tongues and in a vulgar manner.

"Tell, the half breed priest, Dante Merrick, not to get comfortable. The fun has just begun. I'm going to slowly kill this little sow. Then I'll slaughter Merrick's little children. He thinks they're safe, but he's wrong. The Nephilim's family will die at my hands."

Then the child coughed and a frog fell to the floor. The possessed teen finally collapsed and was unconscious.

The End

Made in the USA
Coppell, TX
15 October 2021

64099617R00059